Wanker's Dozen Gang Bang Anthology

12 Gang Bang, Group Sex, Bukkake, Interracial, and BDSM Stories

Hannah Butler

Copyright © 2024, all rights reserved.

These stories are a work of fiction and all characters are 18 or older.

This is intended for adults only!

Contents

Surprise Birthday Gangbang:
An Erotic 3-on-1, Double Penetration,
All Holes Filled, Gangbang Story

I could feel the cold wind on my naked body and hear the honking of cars below as I stood, clasping the railing, my husband kissing my neck and holding my hips. His body heat warmed my back, his hands rubbing my nipples, warming them up just to let them cool in the free air. Even though the sounds of the traffic below would muffle any sounds, I tried to stop them out of instinct but I couldn't help but let a few soft moans leave my throat. When I had woken up this morning, blindfolded, I panicked for a moment, until my husband reassured me to just trust him, that he had a special birthday surprise in store for today.

He knew I was a little bit of an exhibitionist, and had always wanted to have a little naughty fun out on our balcony. We were too high up for anyone to really see without binoculars or a telescope, but even the feeling of being naked outside was enough to turn me on. He slowly rubbed his erect dick against my wetness, teasing the opening without actually penetrating. His rough hands were kneading my 38DD breasts, groping my curvy ass, moving my long blonde hair out of the way so our bodies could rub skin to skin. He grabbed my hips, slowly turning me around and getting me to my knees, rubbing his cock against my tits before tracing my lips with the head, which I quickly and greedily took it in my mouth. I loved having his tool in my mouth, I couldn't take all 8 inches of it but I could get close, and he loved when I tried.

There was no time wasted for me to get up to speed, him gently thrusting against my head as it bobbed up and down his cock, poking down my throat with every thrust, my lips wrapping slightly tightly around as we worked against each other to get his dick as far down my throat as we could. He reached down to tug at my nipple with one hand, holding my head and pulling it toward him with the other. My cunt was dripping now, my body temperature rising as his dick spread my throat open more and more with every increasingly rough piston-like thrust he delivered me. He shoved himself down as far as he could go, holding himself there as he pulled my hair, his loud moans barely audible over the sound of the street below, leaving it there until I was begging for air before pulling it out.

He helped me up as I caught my breath, my chin covered in saliva and my pussy soaking wet, so hot even the blowing wind could only chill it slightly. I was begging him to fuck me between gasps of air, and he wasted no time in lifting my leg up and over the railing, holding me tight, and slamming his cock in from behind. His thickness always made him the best lover I ever had, and he reminded me of this with every thrust, over and over. I couldn't help but moan louder with every moment, my breasts bouncing with every thrust, pleasure shooting throughout my body as he slammed into me roughly, yet only barely satisfying my lust.

I was going crazy, his dick felt so good, the sound of the city below and the chilled wind blowing reminding me entirely of just how exciting this situation was. And yet, I needed more, my body was yearning to swallow ever more of his magnificent cock. I was slamming my body against his, matching him thrust-for-thrust to get him as deep in as possible, to get him to fill my body with his tool. I needed him to give me all his lust, every inch of his body he could, I kept stretching and twisting my body against his, hoping I could get fucked even a little harder. I could feel my pleasure building up quick, but it seemed like he wasn't even beginning. My head spun with the lust, the pleasure, the entire sensation of being treated like such a slut and wanting to be even sluttier. I could barely contain myself anymore, even after he bent me down and picked up speed, ramming me with what could have been every muscle in his body, and I could barely take it. I screamed and moaned as he fucked me, thankful that the trucks below were there to cover up the sound of my orgasm, my pussy being plowed hard sending wave after wave of pleasure through my sensitive cunt. He pulled himself out, got me on my knees, and I could feel his seed shoot across my tits, glazing them and warming them, drizzling down to cover my nipples. That's when he removed the blindfold. I saw the building across from us, with two young college students sitting and jerking off to our little show. I wondered how much they saw, if they were watching when I was choking on his cock or when I was cumming from how well my husband was fucking me, but I did know they saw me now, covered in jizz and panting in the post-orgasmic bliss.

I looked up at my husband as he looked at me, then he made a surprising move: He looked at the two guys and called them over. I had no idea what to think; I hadn't had sex with anyone but my husband since we started dating 5 years ago, and I never thought I would. Here we are, though, with my husband inviting two complete strangers over with no apparent intention other than to let them fuck me. Before I even had too much of a chance to think about it, the doorbell rang and they were here. I was still dirty with my husband's cum on me, welcoming in these two guys who neither of us knew, but were about to fuck me, hopefully until I went crazy. They were staring bewildered, as if they thought they were in a dream, but obviously aroused with the tents in their pants.

They seemed to be more nervous than us, so I tried to break the ice with them a little bit. All I could think of to say was a joking, "I guess you boys liked the show!" with a soft giggle. They nodded their heads, and my husband chuckled as well as he took a seat on a nearby chair, pulling me backwards into his lap.

"You know boys," he said, "when you have a hot, wet, ready woman in front of you, you shouldn't waste any time." Then he picked me up, lowered my ass onto his dick (luckily his dick was still slick with my juices so it went in without too much pain), and spread my legs to drape them over his knees, my entire body exposed to these two who I barely knew, them watching me getting fucked in the worst way as they themselves disrobed fully and closed in to join in almost as if by instinct. Their hands roamed all over my body, groping my tits, pinching my nipples (which my husband loved as I tightened my ass whenever they did it), rubbing my still-drenched slit, all the while my husband slammed himself up into my ass harder and rougher.

I couldn't take just being watched and touched anymore; I needed them inside of me. I grabbed the dick of the guy closest to my head, gently pulled him over, and leaned over my husband's shoulder to take this new cock in my mouth. He definitely wasn't as big as my husband in any way, but I didn't care, I just needed to wrap my lips around hard dick, feel it slide down my throat. I swallowed it down as best I could, my throat still stretched from my husband, I moaned at the sheer sensuality of the situation unfurling around me. I reached my free hand down, rubbing my slit with my middle finger as the two surrounding fingers spread my twat open. I curled my finger in a come hither motion, inviting the stranger into my most private place, and it wasn't long before he made his way in. His cock was definitely shorter, but his girth seemed the same if not thicker than my husbands. If he was still nervous, I never would have known as he quickly picked up the pace and thrust into me when my husband bounced my ass up, pulling out when I was slammed down, both my husband and the stranger alternating pounding my ass and pussy. I kept sucking down the tool in my mouth, it sliding down my throat easily. I alternated between deep throating it and sliding it out to tease the tip with my tongue, which this man seemed to love judging from his moans. I let him start to fuck my face himself, wanting to focus on feeling all these hot cocks pumping in me from every direction. One ultra-thick man in cunt, my husband's huge tool pounding my asshole, and one more stranger having his way with my throat... I was in heaven, getting hornier by the second and being fucked harder even quicker. The strangers couldn't keep their hands off of my tits, squeezing, groping, and pinching at them roughly. All I could hear was lustful moans and slapping skin, my own moans being stifled before they can even begin. I was their fuck toy, nothing I could do could change that even if I had wanted to. I was in this for the long haul until I was either covered in or filled with hot loads of semen. I felt my husband spank my thigh a few times, in rhythm with his fucking, causing me to tense up even more. I couldn't handle it anymore, and with a few accompanying screams had my second orgasm that day, one of the most intense ones I've ever had, which certainly was helped by the men surrounding me only pumping into me harder as I came.

To my surprise, my husband came first among the guys, his seed shooting deep into my ass. He always said he was weak to it, and true enough he always had trouble lasting long during anal. Even so, I wasn't expecting these strangers to outlast him, and soon enough I was being split roasted by these two men I didn't even know. Every time I thought they were getting ready to shoot their load, they'd slow down, or they'd pull out and tease my body. They seemed so nervous before, but now they've turned into experts, treating this like a porn set where they couldn't cum until directed. For my part, my body loved every moment of this tag team fucking, pleasure overwhelming me several times over the next two hours as they had their way with me. Finally, they pulled out of me, helped me sit up, and surrounded me before shooting their hot seed all over my face. It almost legitimately feeling like my entire face was covered with their huge, thick loads. I could barely move at all, just lying back and panting in my post-coital bliss as they rested in some nearby chairs. My husband had brought them out a beer each, and they sat around me talking about who knows what while they watched over me, my body covered in their cum.

Before too long, though, my husband helped them to the door, and after exchanging pleasantries, helped me into the bathroom to get me cleaned up. After I got out of the bath, he kissed me while whispering into my ear, asking me how I enjoyed my birthday. I couldn't lie, I had loved every second of it, and I told him such. He told me he was glad I enjoyed it so much, because those guys wanted to make this a regular thing. He didn't mind sharing me if I didn't mind being shared, and now that he knew I didn't, he was ready to make every day as great as my best birthday ever.

Frat House Gangbang:
How Me and My Boys Gangbanged a Random Girl with another Stranger

Ok, so let me tell you about what happened a few weeks ago during one of our frat parties. It was me and my boys Luke and Jojo. We were really having a great time and drinking up a storm. At about 2am, we went upstairs looking for a restroom. I opened one of the hallway doors thinking it was a restroom and discovered this dude banging this hot petite blonde doggie style. I watched from the doorway as he pounded her hard. He reached over and grabbed one of her tiny b cup breast and gave her nipple a quick pinch. She roughly squeezed the pillow next to the headboard as I noticed her knuckles turning white. WHAP! WHAP! WHAP! The unmistakable sound of pubic and ass colliding.

The guy realized us standing in the doorway. Without the least bit of surprise he looked at us and gave this big shit eating grin. This, to me, was an invitation like no other. I walked closer to let my bros in the room. JoJo closed the door behind him. Luke took his smartphone out and hit his video record app. We were not letting this night go unremembered. As the flash from the phone turned on, the blonde looks up and bites her lower lip and closed her eyes.

She definitely had her own share of drinks tonight. I unbuttoned my jeans, pulled them down, and walked within arms-length of her side. I reached down and felt her firm breast and perky nipples between my fingers. I grabbed her forearm and directed her hand towards my slowly hardening penis. JoJo, pants already off, got on the bed and knelt directly in front of her. This night was going to be great.

Without hesitation, she grabbed JoJo's cock and angled her head towards his dick. She started to suck. Bouncing forward every time the other guys cock went deep in her. I spat on my head to help lubricate my dick as she started to stroke. This went on for no more than a few minutes before JoJo pulled away.

Like clockwork and without a single word spoken, we all changed positions. I walked up to her head as the other guy flipped her to her back. He walked over the other side as JoJo stuck his dick in her soaked pussy. I slapped my dick on the side of her cheek to gain her attention. She quickly turned her head and took my penis in her mouth all while stroking the other guy off. I thrusted to get it in further, feeling her tongue and teeth wrapped around my dick.

Minutes went by as I noticed JoJo's face begin to wince. In one swift motion he pulled out and ejaculated on her perfectly trimmed landing strip. He then took the corner bed sheet and wiped it off her pubes. I pulled out and took over his position. Her pussy, still wet, was truly like warm apple pie. I used my thumb and rubbed her clit like a game controller. The stranger then put his cock in her mouth. Minutes later, I felt her body stiffen up and begin to shake. Her muffled moans getting louder. As she came, the guy pulled out and began to stoke his cock on top of her face. Tongue out, she waited for his semen.

I felt my body begin to tingle and my hair begin to raise. I pulled out just in time as cum hit the side of her inner thigh. I finished the experience with a few strokes with my hand. I found a dry spot on the blanket, wiped her up and got off the bed. The stranger, not yet cuming, flipped her back over to her knees and began to fuck her like a dog. As I pulled up my pants, Luke stopped the recording and began walking out the door. I couldn't resist giving her tits another firm squeeze before leaving the room. No word was ever spoken, and we never saw the couple again.

Melissa and Gina Hook Up With Three Guys:
A Gangbang, Group Sex, Double Penetration Story

After a long night of dancing and drinking at the club, the two girls walk out of the club together. As they hailed a cab, they said good bye to each other.

"I had a great time!" Gina said to Melissa as they stumbled in the taxi. Before Melissa could shut the door, the gorgeous guy that had been dancing with Melissa and buying her drinks all night got in the cab with them, "Where are you girls going?"

"Home…" Melissa replied.

The man gave the cab driver an address, "the party's not over girls." The man began to kiss Melissa and his hands were on Gina's thighs. Melissa pulled away for a second, looked at Gina, "You wanna do this?"

"Let's go!" The cab ride wasn't too long. The whole way, the man and Melissa were kissing, while he felt the warmth and moistness coming from in between Gina's legs. They went inside the house. And the man led both girls into a bedroom.

"You girls want a drink?"

"Sure, make us something strong." The man went into the kitchen to make drinks for the girls, when a text came in on his phone.

He texted back, "I am at home bro, with the two girls from the club. Will leave door open if you wanna join the party."

When the man came back into the room with the drinks, the two girls were both naked on his bed.

Melissa is bent over busy licking in between Gina's legs. "We got started without you," Gina told the man. Melissa is sucking on Gina's clit and licking around her wet cunt. The man put the drinks down, and quickly stripped off his clothes.

"You want to taste what you were feeling on the whole way here?" Melissa asked. She turned towards the man, and put her wet juicy lips around his cock. The man's face is just inches away from Gina's pink wet cunt. He used his index finger to feel her plump pussy lips, then he parted it to see her clit. He flicked it with his tongue, first slowly. Gina squirmed under him, and he flicked is tongue faster against her clit. Gina arched her pelvis up, and the man sucked and nibbled on her clit. Melissa has his cock deep in her mouth. He could feel her tongue rolling around his cock as she sucked. He could even feel her put his balls in her mouth. Her mouth felt so nice and wet.

Then Melissa said, "Let me get a taste of her some more." She moved right in between Gina's legs and began to lick her pussy. This time, she used her fingers inside her. The man can see Melissa is quite moist herself. He got behind her and started to rub his cock against her. Melissa, bent over eating Gina's cunt, moved her legs apart to let him go inside her. He slowly stuck his cock inside Melissa tight cunt. Slowly, inside, her tight wet cunt. Melissa is all out finger fucking Gina, while sucking on her clit. Gina's moans of pleasure was getting louder. The man couldn't help but start fucking Melissa harder. Her ass bounced as he pounded his cock in and out of her.

Fucking Melissa, Melissa licking up Gina's pussy juice. Then she slowed everything down. "We have all night!" Melissa pulled away from the man.

She took his cock, covered with her cunt juice, "Hmmm, let me taste my cunt juice." And put his cock in her mouth. Then Melissa, held Gina's legs open and guided the man's cock into her pink slit. Gina laying on the bed, Melissa straddled her, and put her cunt in front of her face. The man slowly stroking his cock in out of Gina's cunt. Oh, it is even tighter than Melissa's pussy. Melissa starts to rub Gina's clit. And Gina's pussy twitched and got even tighter with every twitch. Just then, the man's friends walked into the house. They heard the door shut.

"Oh, my buddies were coming by, I forgot." the man said to the girls. Without stopping.

"We don't mind, the more the merrier." Melissa said. Two guys walked into the room. "We got started without you guys, so you all just have to come and join us." The two guys got naked and came onto the bed. Melissa went to one of them, and Gina went to the other. They started to suck their dicks, while the other man finger fucked both pussies. He had two fingers inside each pussy... one on the left, the other on the right. While they sucked his friends cocks. Melissa moved her ass down onto the man's cock. Squatting down on it, slowly, his cock went in her ass hole. Melissa laid back on the man. Her legs wide open.

His friend looked at her wide open cunt. Gina reached over and began to rub Melissa's cunt. As Melissa grinded on the man's cock, Gina, put her face down on her friends cunt and began to lick and suck on her clit. One of the man's friend in now behind Gina fucking her.

"I don't want you to feel left out" Melissa said to the other friend. " I need another cock inside me. This bitch's tongue is nothing compared to big fat cock." Gina held one of Melissa's leg up while the other man stuck his cock in her pussy. Both man slowly moved in and out of Melissa.. her ass, her pussy, Melissa was moving along. Gina watched her friend get fucked by the two men. She moved away from the man fucking her. Turns to him and says..

"Fuck her in the mouth." The third man, stuck his cock in Melissa's mouth. She could taste Gina's cunt juices.

"Ohhhhh… yes… Fuck me…" Just then all three men began to go deep and hard fucking Melissa.

"You like that, take all three of them hun," Gina coached. Melissa was enjoying every cock.

Barely Legal Gangbang:
Teen Gets Ravished in all Holes
and Receives Bukkake at a Barely Legal Party!

Rachel received her college acceptance letter the day after her 18th birthday. She was so excited to tell her boyfriend, Shane, because she thought they were going to University together. Unfortunately for Rachel, Shane didn't tell her that he had decided to go to a private school she hadn't applied to. Shane broke up with Rachel three days before graduation. He had been Rachel's first real boyfriend. They lost their virginity together. Rachel was devastated from the breakup. She felt cheated and empty, and she wanted some way to get back at Shane, but she just didn't know how. She needed something to tear her away from the empty pit in her stomach, the hollow and sinking feeling that was ruining every possible thought of excitement at going away to college.

For weeks she just felt depressed and stopped spending time out with the girls. Finally fed up with Rachel's pity party, her best friend Denise forced Rachel to attend a huge bash at their classmate's house. There would be no parents, and everyone was supposed to get good and drunk to celebrate the closing of a chapter and new beginnings. Besides, Denise argued, if Rachel dressed up as hot as possible she could make Shane jealous if he showed up. That was what Rachel really needed to hear. She decided that she'd dress up like she'd never dressed up before.

The night of the party, Rachel started getting ready early. She shaved her toned, mulatto legs and her tight young twat. She waxed her eyebrow and her lip. She did everything she could think of to prep her thin, teenage body. She knew she wanted to go have fun, and screwing around with some stranger at a party seemed like a good opportunity to shove what Shane was missing back in his face. Rachel slipped a lace bra over her perfect little handful, 32B tits. She grabbed a loose fitting t-shirt that showed off more than the straps and the shortest skirt she owned; something that barely came down past the bottom of her taught, bubbly little ass cheeks.

She admired herself in the mirror and knew that if her mother saw her in this outfit, she'd be appalled. Rachel lifted her mini-skirt up an inch and double checked the clean job she'd done on her smooth, young pussy. She felt dirty, and a little tingly all down her spine, contemplating her plan to let a stranger have her tonight. Rachel slowly slipped a finger between her caramel mounds and ran it back and forth in her slit. She watched herself carefully in the mirror as she began pinching and twisting her little pink clit. She was getting lost in the pleasure when suddenly Denise honked her car horn in the driveway.

Rachel yanked her skirt down, grabbed her clutch, and ran for the door to meet Denise. The girls small talked on the way to their classmate's house. When they arrived, the party was already in full swing with tanked teens dancing and making out on the lawn. They made their way inside and immediately were offered drinks by a group of guys. Rachel recognized one of the boys as the older brother of her classmate Richard. He introduced himself, said his name was Dan, and asked if she or Denise wanted to dance. Denise winked at Rachel and gave her a little push forward. She took Dan's hand and he led her to the middle of the living room by the speakers. They ground and jiggled with each other to the thumping bass. Dan said he was a sophomore at the state university and Rachel asked him questions about college life. They danced and talked and drank for twenty or so minutes before Rachel caught an unexpected site out if the corner of her eye. Denise was sitting on a boy's lap on the couch, her pants around her ankles, eyes rolled back in her head as she feverishly ground some boy's pole deep into her pussy. Rachel was shocked at her friend's open display and couldn't take her eyes off of her friend's peach fuzz covered cunt, working some random boy's cock like a seasoned pro. Rachel felt herself getting a little worked up from the display and the grinding dance.

She sent Dan to refill their drinks and gulped her cup down as soon as he returned. She turned herself around and bent over, shoving her lightly exposed ass cheeks into Dan's crotch. She ground on Dan harder than before while enjoying Denise's spectacle on the couch. Rachel felt herself getting wet, stimulated by the sex show and the feeling of Dan's growing tent rubbing into her ass crack, the fabric of his jeans roughly caressing her asshole. Dan placed his hands on her back and started grinding harder, realizing what Rachel was staring at. They both looked on, mesmerized as the stranger grabbed Denise's shoulders firmly and thrust his cock up into her violently while pulling her horny body down to his balls. The boy cried out louder than the music while he emptied his swollen sack into Denise's hungry cunt, cum flowing out of her hole and all over the couch with each hot spurt.

No one else at the party even seemed to notice, but Dan's throbbing dick was starting to push the front of his jeans into Rachel's taught asshole. She looked back at Dan pleadingly, and he grabbed her by the hand. Dan rushed Rachel upstairs to the first bedroom they found. Inside were six or seven drunk party-goers. As much as Rachel didn't really want to put on a show, she was too hot to care. She plopped down at the edge of the bed and hiked her skirt up to her waist. Rachel's pussy lips glistened with her juices for all to see as Dan practically tore the zipper off of his pants. His swollen pole jumped out of his fly as he lined up between Rachel's quivering thighs. A few of the drunk teens in the room cheered him on as he drove all seven inches of his dick into Rachel with no mercy. She let out a whimper as his body slammed into her.

Shane had never been that rough with her before, and she wasn't quite sure if she liked it. Her eager body didn't care, though. Her pussy started clenching down on Dan's thrusting cock, her hips pumping to meet him. She laid back completely on the bed and surrendered to the punishment. She closed her eyes and started relishing the smack of Dan's hips into hers. She felt her body getting hotter and hotter as each thrust threatened to tear her apart. She was wriggling and moaning on the bed while the whole room watched Dan grunting and pounding away at her. Rachel was startled when two of the onlookers suddenly grabbed her arms and held them pinned out at the edges of the bed. The room got louder, cheering Dan on to finish her like a man. Dan grabbed Rachel's legs and pushed them together, then up to her chest. He was getting into her deeper then Shane ever had. She felt a little embarrassed because she realized she was about to orgasm on display; but above anything else she felt hot like never before.

She could feel the tip of Dan's cock hitting all the way to the back of her pussy and she was about to lose it in front of a room full of strangers. Dan started moaning loudly as he ground himself deep in her sopping cunt. Hot spurt after spurt of his cum jabbed at the back of her pussy, sending her over the edge. As Dan unloaded all of his pent up urge into her tiny, teenage body, Rachel moaned deep and started shaking vigorously. The two strange boys pinning down her arms held her tight as she squirmed and wriggled and screamed in ecstasy. Dan pulled his softening member out of her cream filled hole and let her legs fall off the edge of the bed while glistening streams of their juices dripped out of her quivering cunt, between her ass cheeks, and onto the floor. Rachel felt satiated like never before as she came down off of her orgasm. She lay still catching her breath, still pinned to the bed. One of the wasted girls in the room got on her knees between Rachel's open thighs; pulling her dripping pussy lips wide open with her long fingernails. Rachel felt a little alarmed at this stranger's presence between her legs, but her body was too tired to really struggle. She felt incredibly nervous about the position she was in, pinned down and exposed. The drunk girl at the foot of the bed dug her tongue deep between Rachel's light brown mounds and connected with her clit, sending shivers through Rachel's spine. The girl sloppily worked Rachel over with her tongue, sucking and toying with her. Rachel relaxed and started enjoying the attention that she was so nervous about just moments before. The girl between Rachel's thighs must have been incredibly drunk because she was having trouble even staying on her knees. After five or ten minutes of the goaded guzzling of Rachel's dripping juices, the girl fell over laughing hysterically with her cum covered mouth. Rachel was surprised at how much she enjoyed the attention from another girl, and she felt her body getting worked up and needy again. She didn't want to ask out loud, but she secretly started hoping Dan would fill her again.

As if in answer to her silent prayer, two more strangers grabbed her legs and held them open, spread eagle in the air. Her ass was pulled just off the end of the bed as she was completely immobilized by these strangers. She hadn't realized it, but word must have spread around the tanked party-goers about the show in the bedroom. The room was jammed wall to wall with people coming to see the spectacle of her beautiful, light brown body getting used. No one seemed to notice Denise's fun earlier, but they were certainly paying attention to her.

Pinned and exposed, Rachel couldn't stand the anticipation of getting Dan again. But Dan didn't answer her body's needs this time. A tall, lean boy saddled himself between her legs and slipped his horny cock straight into her hungry pussy. Rachel came to the party expecting to fool around with someone, but she had never imagined that the whole party would come to fool around with her. She thought about crying out to stop the intrusion, but her body was betraying her. Worked up by the drunk girl, she desperately needed to be fucked. She relaxed and started thrusting her hips into this new boy as hard as she could from her captive position. The party-goers cheered as this newcomer plowed her with all his might, rattling the bed against the wall. Rachel moaned and quivered and shook as she kept trying to get his stiff rod deeper and deeper into her. She wanted desperately to cum like she had just before. The room was filled with the noise of shouted encouragements and the loud smacking of her sloppy pussy being smashed into the boy's open fly. The boys holding her legs pulled them apart farther than before and Rachel screamed as she felt like she was being torn in two. Her pussy was completely vulnerable to this boy's assault. She kept trying to meet his thrusts, but she was too restricted now. She lay still and enjoyed the feelings coming from deep within her as the boy used her pussy like a toy.

She could feel herself getting close again, but the stranger between her legs pulled out before she could make it. He sprayed cum all over her skirt and shirt as the room went nuts with laughter and applause. Rachel had forgotten about the crowd in her heat, though. She was begging loudly, crying at the top of her lungs for someone to finish her. The drunk, horny boys surrounding her were more than happy to oblige. One of them jumped up on the bed and shoved his hard cock into her begging mouth. Another got between her stretched legs and jammed his fat cock home into her cunt. She moaned loudly on the dick in her mouth as both boys started fucking away at her welcoming holes. Rachel came hard at the sensations of both boys at once, moaning and gagging against the cock in her mouth while her shaking body tried milking the boy between her legs.

After what seemed like an eternity spent in her orgasm, she re-laxed while the boys tore away at her. Eventually both of them started to cum hard, putting on a show for the crowd. She gulped down cum as fast as she could while she felt her pussy being filled to the brim with seed. Her body felt like it was on fire from the hot sensations coursing through her. She cried out for relief from the heat, and party-goers obliged their new plaything. People started stuffing ice cubes from their drinks in Rachel's abused pussy and up her exposed ass-hole. She shook and whimpered at the freezing feelings inside her, water and cum dripping from her body. One boy stuffed his hand against her sopping cunt, and rubbed the mixture of juices all over his cock. Then, he started smearing them all over her wet asshole. The boys holding Rachel lifted her up, and this boy climbed beneath her on the bed. As they lowered her back down, he guided her tight ass-hole to the head of his cock. Rachel squirmed a bit at the thought of being taken up the ass. It was something that Shane has asked for, and she had never been willing to deliver. Now, she was going to let a stranger pierce her bum.

She could only imagine Shane's surprised face if he knew. The team holding her started pushing her body down and she felt her ass-hole resist this stranger's cock. She tried to relax as much as she could and finally felt her hole spread open. White fire sprung through her body in a searing combination of pleasure and pain as the boys forced her down onto this long pole. She felt her skin tug and release, tug and release, over and over again as she was lowered down. She kept kicking and squirming and moaning as waves of pleasure and pain gnawed at her brain. She had never felt so full. Rachel felt like she was impaled on a good five or six inches of dick, and the crowd around her cheered with sexual excitement.

Quickly, another boy scampered up on the bed and stuffed her mouth with his dick, and a third got in position between her caramel thighs. The crowd counted down from three, and at one the boy with the tip of his cock at her cunt lips plunged himself into her. She tried to cry out at the sensation of being fucked up her ass and pussy at the same time, but the massive rod in her mouth stifled any noise. The crowd whooped and cheered as all three boys started laying into her. She was completely filled. Both cocks rubbing at her inner walls between her legs was too much for her. Other boys weren't going to wait their turns now that she was completely occupied. The two boys holding her arms down reached over and grabbed her shirt collar. They ripped her t-shirt in two, exposing her heaving chest and delicious black bra. While the three boys worked over her holes, the boys holding her arms down grabbed her bra and ripped it from her tits. The hooks and fabric scratched welts into Rachel's back and sides as the bra was tossed away. She was losing control of her body from the assault and barely noticed the new pain. Boys from around the room, turned on like never before by the sight of this goddess being used in every hole, started jacking off and covering her scrumptious, Hershey kiss nipples in spurt after red hot spurt of cum.

Rachel's eyes rolled back in her head while she gagged on the mammoth cock in her mouth. Her body began quivering in the pit of her stomach. The double onslaught between her legs drove her teen body to cum. Her asshole tightened, her pussy started squeezing its cock, and her whole body let loose. She started squirting her juices all over the stranger's throbbing dick that was ramming her pussy relentlessly. She came fiercely, her cunt juices being forced down this boy's rod, coating the balls of both boys tearing her asshole and pussy apart. Rachel's head began to swim from the overtaking pleasure, and she completely collapsed, passing out from the strain on her tender body. Rachel awoke in the morning to an empty room, on a stranger's bed, with no idea how many boys and girls had used her sore body. Her asshole was puckered and bruised. Warm, sticky cum was still dribbling out from between her caramel mounds. Her clothes were torn and stained. Her face and tits were a sticky, jizz-covered mess. She reeked of stale sex and all she could taste was spunk. She had no idea what happened to her after that last orgasm, but what she did know was that she couldn't wait to go to University anymore. She lusted greedily at the idea of college parties and what tantalizing new sensations they might bring.

No Limits College Gangbang:
An Erotic Story with Double Penetration, Groupsex, Bukkake, and More!

Amy held up a finger and the roar of the party quieted down as all attention fell on her. She tilted her head back and opened her mouth. A white colored cum bubble formed between her lips as she slowly blew out until it popped. She scrunched up her eyes and flecks of the bubble remained on her face as all the guys and a few of the more fun loving girls in the room cheered her on. Amy gave a small bow that was accentuated by her D cup breasts.

"Thank you. I'd like to thank Aaron for his delicious cum. Without him, none of this would have been possible," she said. She grabbed Aaron's hand and held it up as if she were declaring the winner of a boxing match. Aaron did look like he could have competed. He was a combination of lean and tall.

For Amy, attending such a sports heavy college, was the perfect hunting ground for her type of guy. She liked trying a new one each week, but at parties like this, she did her best to try as many as possible. She gave Aaron a slap on the ass.

"You did good, kid. Now who's next?" The blond girl with the perky D cup breasts looked around the room and locked on to one guy who had been brave enough to pull out his dick and stroke it while he watched her give a naked blow job.

"Come here," she stepped past a few people who had crowded around. One of the guys wasn't too subtle about reaching out to touch her breast.

"Can I take my turn now?" he asked. Amy put a hand over his and squeezed over his fingers. Her ass pressed against his hips and she could feel a hardening cock pressing up against her cheeks.

"Mmmm, easy there big guy. I've got my eye on a cock already. Maybe you had been beating your meat instead of your beers then I would have picked you next," she teased. She continued past him, but not before taking his drink out of his hand and finishing it off.

Brad's pants were around his ankles. He hadn't bothered to wear any boxers. Amy had a bit of a reputation at these parties. He had come for one reason, and that reason had just dropped to her hands and knees and was crawling the last few feet to him. Brad pulled his foot out of his pants and kicked the jeans off.

"Meow," said Amy. She shook her bare ass and leaned forward to lick the length of Brad's cock. On her second lick she started from his sack. Her hand wrapped around the head and her tongue dragged along all eight inches of his cock till she reached the tip. She had been pushing back on the cock as she held it, but at the tip she let go and the cock slapped her face. The watching crowd cheered her on. Amy's college nights might not be filled with much studying, but she was defiantly learning how to be a performer.

"Oh, fuck, that feels good." Brad put a hand on Amy's head and pushed her down on the tip. He felt some resistance.

"My jaw is a bit sore from the last guy, so you've lucked out. I'm going to stuff this bad boy into my cunt." Amy licked her lips and spit on the cock. She brought herself to a standing position by pushing down on each of Brad's knees.

"I'll pound your pussy. Just bring it a little closer," said Brad. Amy turned around and took a step back to straddle him. She reached down and guided the head of his cock to her slit.

Amy sat down on his cock and leaned back so that her back touched his chest. She brought up a hand to his head and titled hers back so that she could whisper into the opposite ear. "No need to be a gentleman. Treat me like your whore. Use me. Make me into that story you tell your friends when you get drunk."

Brad felt his cock being squeezed inside of Amy. He forgot about the rest of the people in the room. He wrapped one arm under Amy's breasts and brought his other hand down to between her legs. He could feel her bouncing up and down on his cock. He pulled her all the way down into his lap and rubbed her clit in circles with his fingers. His breath came in low grunts. He moved his ass back against the couch and then thrust back up into Amy.

To her credit, she didn't take long to cum. Amy brought her own hands to her breasts and pinched her nipples as she squirted on his cock. Her loud moans brought the room to a silence once more.

When everyone had stopped talking there was one sound that could be heard. It was of Brad's skin slapping Amy's as he bent her over and continued to pound her pussy.

Amy's hands touched the ground not that far away from her feet. She lifted her head and gave it a shake to clear some of her blond hair that had been obscuring her vision. Several people had their cell-phones out and pointed at her. She gave a weak smile, but found it hard to concentrate with a hard cock sill ramming her pussy. She wanted to get up, but her legs were too shaky. A hand picked her up by the arm and helped her back up into Brad's lap.

"I've finished drinking," said the guy from earlier. Where Amy usually preferred the tall and lean, she also had a special lust for the tall and muscular. It didn't help quell her lust that after helping her up onto a cock, he brought her hand to where his was.

"Give it to me," gasped Amy. She unzipped his khakis and put her hand inside his pants. She could barely hold onto the meat inside. Amy caught her breath in her throat when she fished the cock out of his pants. "Fuck turns. I want this now."

Amy's jaw creaked as she went further down the strong man's cock. She reached around to his ass cheeks and sank her finger nails into his flexed ass. The cock in her pussy continued to pound up into her. Each thrust shook her body as well as her tits. It was a show all would have paid to have seen. After reaching the clean shaven base of the cock, Amy pulled it all the way out and held onto it like a crutch.

"Who want's to fuck my ass?" She yelled. The loudest response surprised many of the guests. It came from the peitie asian hostess of the party.

"I'll wreak that asshole," she shouted. The people around her backed away and she stood alone when her eyes met Amy's. Amy was riding a sexual high and the small girl's offer was the most appealing by far.

"Lisa, right?" Amy didn't break eye contact with the woman, but after asking her question she quickly licked the cock in her hand. Li-sa's answer was drowned out by the loud popping noise made when Amy sucked on the tip.

"Let's go to your room."

More offered to join and Amy agreed to anyone who had enough courage to get naked in the room in front of the rest of the party. When Amy later watched several of the videos taken by the people who had gone to the party, she counted around ten naked people in Lisa's bed room.

Brent had the best position out of all the guys. Amy rode him reverse cowgirl. This left her open to lean over the edge of the bed and suck cock as her hips bounced up and down on Brent's dick. Lisa, who Amy wish she had spent more time touching in hind sight after watching the videos, was straddling Brent's stomach with her strap on vibrator. Whenever Brent's hands were not on Amy, they were feeling up Lisa's tiny ass. The strong man, who had been one of Aaron's friends, held onto Amy's head and fucked her face in front of six other naked guys and a few others who were recording.

Amy didn't mind the face fucking. She was glad he had taken over slamming his meat down her throat while her searching hands found a cock waiting for each one. Her hands slid up and down the cocks and scooped up whatever precum on the tips she could find to use as lube on the rest of the shaft. Amy didn't have words for the vibrating beast that was in her ass. It vibrated so hard that she was certain even Brent could feel it though the small amount of flesh that separated the two holes.

She could feel the hostess's hands on her as she rammed the false cock into her ass. The small girl grabbed at Amy's breasts and would pinch her nipples. Amy's steady stream of grunts and moans grew stronger with each pinch. The bodies became slick as the intense heat of so many naked bodies pushed everyone's endurance to the limit.

Aaron's friend was the first to give. He shoved his cock way past Amy's gagging point and flooded her throat with cum. She jerked and twitched while she struggled to swallow it all. He pulled out of her mouth and Amy had only a moment's rest to catch her breath before another cock was pressed to her lips. She tried to look up to see who it was, but it felt like her other senses were dimming as overflowing pleasure was edging them out.

The next one to cum was from her right hand. She felt the man cum in spurts and by the second one, they were all landing on her back. She didn't need to look back to know it was Lisa's hand that was rubbing the cum into her skin. She couldn't look back. All she could see when she had her eyes open was the hips of the man in front of her.

Brent held on like a champ. She felt him cum inside her. He stayed hard and, given how daunting a task it would have been to switch him out, she was thankful. Lisa would always find where each man had come on Amy and then rub it into a different area of Amy's exposed skin. She was covered from her finger tips to her shoulders. From her back to her ass. Lisa made sure to save an especially heavy load to rub into Amy's tits.

Amy rode each orgasm she had like she was caught in the riptide of the ocean. As soon as one seemed to end, the pleasure had built up so high that it tugged her back down into a carnal haze of spasiming muscles and uncontrollable grunts. She felt full and hungry at the same time. Her hunger drove her on as she drank every drop of cum that was shot into her mouth.

It was Lisa who put an end to the gang bang. She was watching Amy closely and, while the girl's hands were still moving on men's cock, she saw that Amy had buried her head at the base of a cock she had been sucking for ten minutes. For the last three of those minutes she hadn't bothered to move her head. Lisa grabbed Amy by the hair and saw that her half lid eyes were a sure sign she was sound asleep.

"Party's over boys. This slut's had enough," she called out. She reached down between her legs and shut off the vibrator. On lookers who were not going to join in had left half an hour ago. All that were left were the horniest of the bunch. Brent lifted Amy off his cock and helped Lisa tuck her into the bed.

"Thanks," he said. "Another hour of this and I'd have to call a doctor." Brent pointed down at his erection.

"I thought a little blue pill might be behind your spectacular per-formance. Seems like someone think's ahead," said Lisa. Her hand drifted down to slowly slide along his cock. Brent's over sensitive cock twitched in her hand.

"I've spent a long time looking at that beautiful ass of yours. Are you up for some fooling around?" he asked.

"Such a romantic. Sorry, I'm not, but I am saddened by the thought that our little whore will be leaving this party without some cum in her ass. I feel like I wouldn't have been a proper hostess if I let that happen." She moved over to Amy's face and caressed it gently.

"Are you for it?" Lisa asked.

Amy rubbed her eyes and arched her back with a stretch. She licked her lips and nodded then rolled over onto her stomach. "Lisa, can you do the rest? I can't move."

Brent got up on the bed once more and lined up his cock with Amy's asshole. Lisa took the cock into her mouth for one sloppy slurp and then pulled it out. A trail of spit connected her mouth to the tip of the cock that she was now working into Amy's well fucked hole.

"Feels like you kept your promise," said Brent. He slid easily into Amy's ass. "You spread this open enough that if feels like a second pussy."

At those words Amy flexed her ass and clamped down on the cock inside her. She kept her face buried in a pillow, but let out a long moan of satisfaction. Lisa moved back to the edge of the bed and grabbed the vibrator from her strap on. She used it to tease her clit as she watched Brent fuck Amy's ass. Brent came moments before Lisa did. He kept his cock in Amy's ass for a minute longer afterwards and when he pulled out he had finally started to soften.

Lisa's orgasm was a culmination of the evening's events. She had ridden her desire to the highest peak she could go and when she reached the top it was like breaking a blanket of clouds and finally being bathed in sunlight. It was by far the strongest orgasm of her life. She rode it down for two minutes before opening her eyes to find the room empty of all men.

Amy was sound asleep beside her and Brent had grabbed his clothes and headed out the door. Lisa got in under the covers and the two slept till mid morning with the lights still on.

Five Black Men for Little White Layla: Interracial Gangbang Erotica with Three Cream Pies and Two Facials

Layla was in her first year of college, and decided to go to the toga dance. She got drunk before going, because she assumed that she wouldn't be able to get any drinks at the party. She, however met a black man, who kept a steady amount of beers coming in, and would grind with her to every song. Layla had always been attracted to black guys, which a lot of people found strange considering she was a white female.

She could feel the black man's hard cock rubbing against her ass, as they continued to dance. The feeling of it pressed against her kept turning her on, and she knew her wetness was growing. Finally he asked her what she had been hoping all night, "would you like to come back to my apartment?" He kind of had devilish smile when he asked.

Layla immediately agreed, and he laughed. The black man adjusted his pants so his boner wasn't apparent, and lead Layla to his apartment. "I'm only a few blocks away," he informed Layla.

"I don't care," Layla drunkenly replied, and latched onto him. She giggled at the thought that she didn't even know his name. She was about to have sex with a stranger she just met at a dance. The thought turned her on even more.

"We're here," the black man smirked, and opened the door. Inside there were about five more black guys all sitting and watching something on TV.

"Hey! Jamal brought us a sexy one tonight!" One of the men shouted. Layla was confused, she wasn't expecting this many men.

Jamal squeezed her hand and whispered in her ear, "Hope you're down for a gangbang."

It had always been one of her fantasies, she just didn't expect it to happen like this. But seeing all the men turned her on even more. She told Jamal, "I'm down."

He laughed again and shouted to everyone, "Let the party begin!"

Jamal pulled Layla's shirt off, and she was surprised at how quickly this started. Next he unclasped her bra, revealing her 32C's to everyone. The men on the couch watched intensely and began rubbing their cocks through their pants. Jamal started squeezing one of her tits, and kissed her roughly. She slid her tongue into his mouth and started rubbing his boner through his jeans.

Jamal stopped kissing Layla and pulled down her pants, and he saw how wet she was already. Her thong was completely soaked. "Girl, you've been ready," he said.

She giggled and got down on her knees. Jamal removed his pants, then his boxers revealing his large black cock. Layla gasped at the size of it, it had to be at least 10 inches. She gently grabbed it and began to jerk it. The other black men stood up and formed a circle around her. They still were rubbing their dicks through their pants.

"Come on bitch, suck it," Jamal ordered. Layla obeyed and wrapped her mouth around the head of his penis.

She started sucking and moving her mouth further down his shaft. She could hardly fit half of his cock in her mouth. He placed his hands on her head, and pulled it more onto his dick. Layla gagged, but attempted to deep throat him even more, and her lips were practically on his balls. She rolled her tongue all over his length, and his balls as well.

Jamal released his grip on her head, and she stopped sucking his cock to get a breather. That's when she noticed the five other black men were undressed and had their cocks out. All of them were around the same size as Jamal. One of them moved forward and rubbed his penis on her shoulder, wanting it to get as hard as Jamal's.

Layla stopped gawking at their cocks, and started blowing Jamal's again. The other men all had their dicks pressed against somewhere on her body. Some of them were slapping their cocks on her, and the others were just humping her. Jamal pulled her head off him, and ordered her to suck the other cocks.

She decided to start with the guy to the right of Jamal, she placed his semi hard dick into her mouth and gently sucked it. Moving her head up and down his shaft. After she got the second guy hard, Jamal ordered the third guy to sit on the couch. Layla followed and started jerking him, her ass was in the air.

Jamal removed her thong and pressed his fingers against her pussy, ensuring it was wet and ready. She started sucking the big black cock she had been jerking. Jamal pushed his dick against her vagina, and with a quick thrust he was inside. Layla gasped and felt her body jerk. Jamal grabbed her hips and began pushing hard inside her.

That was when she realized he wasn't wearing a condom. She was too drunk to care though, and kept moving her mouth up and down the cock. Layla moaned with pleasure. Jamal thrusted himself even deeper inside Layla, causing her to gasp again. The man she had been sucking was fairly hard and stood up, allowing the next black dude to sit down.

Jamal was grunting now, "I'm going to cum inside you, you slut."

Layla was about to protest, but it was too late. With a final grunt, Jamal held onto her hips and pushed deep inside her and held his cock there. She felt the hot cum fill deep inside her and it caused her to orgasm. Layla screamed with pleasure. The next guy immediately began rubbing his cock against her pussy. Jamal pushed the black man's cock she was sucking out of the way. "Clean my dick off," he ordered Layla.

As soon as she began licking and sucking Jamal's cock, the second guy penetrated her. He didn't feel as good as Jamal, but it was making her orgasm last even longer. Once she finished cleaning Jamal's cock off, another guy sat down for her to suck. Layla licked his hairy balls, and he gripped her hair then forced her to go down deep onto his penis. The second guy was thrusting hard now, and she could tell he already was so close to cumming. She was surprised how some men couldn't last that long.

While she was still giving head, one of the black guys slapped his hard dick against her face, and started rubbing it on her cheek. She could feel some precum being spread against her face. The man fucking her began speeding up, and held himself deep inside her as Jamal had done, and released his semen inside her. Layla couldn't help but moan again, as she was filled. She felt multiple loads from this guy shooting inside her. As he pulled out, some of the cum started to drip down her pussy.

The next man didn't wait even a second, and started fucking her. Layla didn't realize how close the black man she was sucking was to cumming. It surprised her when his hot load filled her mouth, and he moaned with pleasure. Thinking quickly she swallowed everything, but she wasn't fast enough, more and more cum kept filling her mouth, and some of it was starting to drip out of her mouth.

Layla knew that the cock of the man fucking her now was probably covered with the other two men's cum, but he didn't seem to care as he continued thrusting inside her. The last black guy she had yet to suck sat on the couch in front of her. Layla rolled her tongue all around the head of his dick. She lightly sucked his tip, before moving her mouth slowly down his cock.

The black man pressed his hands on her head and started pushing her faster on his cock. The man fucking her decided to follow what the other two guys had done, and announced, "I'm cumming inside you also bitch." He held onto her and cum started spurting out of his cock. So much had already filled her, that cum started flowing out of her pussy, running down his balls.

Layla started orgasming again, and as her vagina tightened around his dick, it seemed to suck even more sperm out of him. He moaned with pleasure, and eventually pulled his limp dick out, wiping the mixture of cum off onto Layla's back.

The man she was blowing said, "I'm going to give you a facial, you little whore, and you're going to enjoy it!" Layla loved facials, the hot cum dripping down her face always would make her orgasm again. The black guy used one hand to grip her hair on the back of her had and the other hand to jerk his dick. She could see his balls tensing up and knew the load was coming. His spunk squirted out of his cock onto her forehead. Then another load onto her cheek. Layla opened her mouth wide, and he blew another load inside there, and finally one last load landed right above her eye. Layla orgasmed one last time.

Six Person Gangbang with a Wife, Four Black Men, and a Husband in Drag: An Interracial, Transsexual, Gangbang, and Humiliation Erotic Story

After a long day at work, the husband walks into the front door of his modest size home. After stepping through the threshold he finds a note next to the door. It reads:

I am upstairs in the bedroom with some company. They have been here with me all day. I would love for you to join us. Go to the downstairs bathroom and read the instructions I have left for you.

Butterflies fill his stomach as he paces down the hall way to the bathroom. He knows that his wife and he have discussed the possibility of sharing her with other men. In the past they have discussed what it would be like to explore with a hot black man.

Both the husband and wife are white and in their late twenties. They have been monogamous for the duration of their six-year marriage. The husband has an average build with an average size cock. However, the wife always jokes about how his average size cock isn't enough for her. She needs a big black cock. The door to the bathroom gives way with a turn of the knob. The directions are laying on a crisp piece of pink paper located on top of a box. The note reads:

Take a shower and shave your face, chest, and legs completely. Once that is done, you may open the box. If you do not shower and shave like I have requested, my boyfriends, yes plural, will throw you out of the house and will not let you back in until they are finished with fucking my brains out.

The dutiful husband shaved his face, head, legs, and chest as requested. He thought it was odd that she had requested that he do so. Then it hit him. As he climbed out of the shower he opened the box and saw a makeup bag and women's clothes. He pulled out each item carefully. Inside the makeup bag were fake press-on nails that were already painted hot pink. There was also red lipstick, mascara, and perfume. The next item to be removed from the box was a bright shiny red blouse. Beneath it he pulled out a black bra with a silky pair of panties bunched up inside of them. He didn't recognize the items in the box except for the panties. They belonged to his wife, and from the scent that they were emitting they were worn today, and she was extremely aroused while wearing them. Inside the box the remaining items were a black leather skirt, fishnet stockings, a black short haired wig, and a pair of black stilettos that have a four-inch heel. The sight of all of what was in front of him made his forget about what exactly what was going on upstairs.

He looked down at his cock and saw the pre-cum dripping, almost like a wet pussy. He has always wanted to wear women's clothes while playing in the bedroom. A handful of times his wife donned a strap on and made him suck it before fucking him in the ass. He began to wonder if she plans on fucking him in front of her boyfriends. He quickly pulled on the clothes that were laid out in front of him and applied the makeup. On the bottom of the box, another note read:

Once you have prettied up, cum join us.

Never walking in high heels before became a quick challenge, especially while walking up the stairs. He didn't know if he was trembling because he was scared of falling down the stairs or trembling because he was excited and afraid of what was behind his bedroom door. From outside the door he could hear moaning and grunting, but couldn't identify how many people might be in his bedroom. The only hint he received was from the note that read plural boyfriends. He pushed the door open to find a dark ass thrusting hard and fast into his wife on the edge of the bed, doggy style. None of the four tall black men or his wife acknowledged him while he walked into the room. The husband, off balance from the heels, was curious to see how his wife was enjoying herself, so he took a few steps toward the side of the bed to see her and her lover from the side. To his astonishment, her dark skinned lover was pounding his huge cock into her ass. She has never even tried anal sex with her husband. The wife looked up at her husband for the first time, smiled, and said, "Do you like the way my boyfriend is fucking my ass with his fucking massive black cock?" As she finished her sentence, her lover began to thrust harder and faster and moaned deep.

"I'm gonna cum again" he said. The husband wondered how many times she was fucked today. Her lover didn't pull out of her ass. The husband noticed that he was not wearing a condom. He unloaded all of his cum into her body. The other guys in the room watched and chuckled a bit. The look on their faces told the husband that they have seen this a few times. When her lover, Mike, finished, he pulled his long thick cock out and the wife rolled over onto her back. "I want you to meet Mike, Randy, Joe, and Tony, my boyfriends. You look pretty, doesn't she boys?"

Mike responded with a laugh, "Ha, maybe a little slutty, but not pretty."

"Don't listen to them," she said. "You look pretty to me. Now come be a good slut and lick up all of this cum from my ass and pussy."

The husband climbed onto the bed and went onto all fours and dropped his face and began licking up all of the cum from her legs, ass, and pussy. "It took you long enough to come home and get ready. They each have fucked me like twice in the last two hours. They all can go a long time, way longer than you ever have. I've been seeing Mike here for a while. He invited his buddies over for us both to play. Sorry, I couldn't wait for you sweetie. Keep licking, I want you to get it all. It has to be like 6 loads down there everywhere. They are all heavy cummers if you couldn't tell. I know because I swallowed two loads while Mike was fucking my ass right now. Hey boys, are you all ready to go again?"

Randy, Joe, and Tony approached both the husband and the wife. Randy and Joe pulled the husband off the bed and forced him to the ground on his knees. Randy shoved his half hard cock into the husband's mouth. Even half hard, he must have been close to eight-inches. The husband has never sucked a cock before, but he loved it. Joe bent down to grab the husband's leather ass.

"You have a nice little bubbly ass. I wonder if it's tight. Would you like me to shove my cock in your ass?" After no response, he chocked the husband and asked again, "Slut, would you like it if I fucked your ass?"

"Yes."

"Get on the bed and go on all fours." The slut climbed onto the bed and Randy laid down in front of him, shoving his nine inches into his mouth. Joe ripped the stockings and slid the panties over. After a little lube being applied, Joe shoved the head of his huge cock into the slut's ass. It was painful at first, but a moment of waiting with just the tip in made the pain go away. The slut loosened his ass and Joe pressed in deep slowly as deep as he could go. It hurt so bad, but felt amazing to the slut. The slut looked over to see Mike and Tony taking turns fucking the wife while she sucked the other. Joe fucked the slut until he was about to pop. He pulled out and told the slut to get on his knees. He came a huge load all over his face and shiny blouse.

"Lick that shit up right now. Clean that shit," Joe said as he pointed as his fresh spunk on the slut. Right as the slut cleaned up the last drop, without warning, Randy stood up and came in the same exact places. The slut tried to swallow all he could. The remainder of the evening was spent with all four men getting sucked and fucking both "women" in the room. The wife thought it would be fun to swap cum a few times. The husband loved making out with his wife while sharing cum. That was the only contact he had with her the entire night.

"I love you my husband, but I think I just want these guys to fuck me from now on. Their cocks feel amazing in my cunt and ass. But don't worry I know you have needs, so I'll allow you to get dolled up like this and get fucked with or without me around. I bought other sexy clothes I would love to see you in. Maybe once in a while, I will play with or lick your clit. But only if my boyfriends have been taken care of first. They have quite and appetite you know. I never knew anyone could cum more than once, let alone multiple times in an afternoon and night. Now be a good wife and make sure all of the boys are cleaned up. I need you to wash the sheets and our clothes too. When that all done and the boys are all gone, maybe I'll take out my strap on and fuck you before bed."

Mysterious BDSM with Four Men

Ashlee looks around nervously, glancing around in the dimly lit room. Her hands are tied tightly onto the wooden planks, her body like Jesus on the cross except for one difference: her legs are tied wide open and held in place by tight bindings. She is beautiful, a long haired brunette with big green eyes behind thick lashes and a mouth with plump pink lips that many women would envy. She has a curvy figure and massive tits with large brown areolas and a fat round ass. Her pussy is hairless and smooth and a delicious shade of pink. She has a soft belly and thick thighs, gorgeous tanned skin all the way down to her perfectly polished toes. She is completely naked and exposed, shaking with fear and trying to remember how she had gotten here.

The last thing Ashlee remembers is that she was at the new bar, the Spore Lung, and a sexy, fit man had approached her with a drink. Just the thought of him walking up to her, and how he had given her that look of desire as he leaned against the bar, made her pussy twitch even in her fear. Something about him drove her crazy. His bald head and muscles weren't usually her type, but he looked powerful and dominant. She began to wonder about his dick, wondering if it would be thick and how the head would look. Just imagining this, she could feel her wetness spread and begin to drip down her thighs. She ached to have even one hand free to stroke her clit and bring release to her arousal. *What am I doing?* she thought.

Suddenly she is aware of someone watching her. Then all of a sudden the light is switched off. She tries to scream, but her mouth is gagged. Then she feels hands on her body. Not just two, but at least eight hands groping her soft full breasts, pinching and teasing her hard nipples, hands on her thighs reaching back and grabbing at her ass. She starts to try and move against her restraints, completely terrified. Then all at once, she moans deep in her throat as a set of lips sucks on to her wet pussy, the tongue gently swirling around her hard aching clit and darting in and out of her hole. With the mystery man kissing and sucking her clit, she can barely stand it. At each breasts, there are two mouths eagerly sucking her hard nipples into their mouths, gently flicking their tongues across, and gently biting. A mouth at the back of her now begins kissing her ass, spreading her cheeks wide cheeks, and using his tongue to begin swirling around her asshole, then probing in. She is completely lost in the feelings. She wants to scream out, "Yes! Eat my ass please! Don't stop sucking my pussy!"

The mouth between her legs licks greedily and sucks her juices that are now flowing even more so. All at once, the gag is removed from her mouth and the plank she is on is lowered to the ground. One by one her restraints are taken off. She reaches out for the bodies around her feeling hard muscle, and her hands finally find what she wants. She gets on her knees and moves toward the hard cock in her hand and begins sucking it hard and fast while she jerks off the other next to her. While sucking away, a mouth has found her pussy again, and she lets out a soft moan and begs, "Please don't stop! Yessss! Yes!"

She can feel the hot cum begin to shoot into her mouth, and she swallows every drop. The now spent cock pulls away as it drips one last drop down her chin. She moves her mouth towards the other cock, this one quite small in comparison, and she begins sucking fast. It doesn't take long for it to explode down her throat. She's on her knees, and the mouth is still there sucking her pussy. She begins fucking back against his tongue, feeling it probe her insides. All at once, the mouth isn't there, and she feels a hard cock placed at her lips. She feels him jerking his cock off and sucks the head in and out of her mouth. He quickly cums, and she feels his hot orgasm drip all over her breasts.

Strong hands grab her waist from behind, pushing her down so her face is to the ground and her ass and exposed pussy are high in the air. His hands grab and spread at her ass then she feels the thickest cock slide into her aching wet slit. She lets out a long moan. It's exactly what she has been craving. The thick cock has completely filled her tight pussy, and it stretches over the enormous head. She begins fucking back towards it, trying to take as much as she can. He grabs her hips and begins slamming into her full length with deep, long, hard strokes. Ashlee is moaning and begging for his cum. She reaches her hand under her and begins rubbing her clit fast as his hard cock pounds her pussy, his balls brushing her hand. She feels a hot explosion deep inside her that sets her off, and her pussy begins throbbing and contracting around the thick cock as she cums all over it. He slides his cock out and his massive load drips out of her pussy and onto her fingers. She takes them to her mouth and sucks them clean. She feels him lay beside her on the hard floor and she can't help but to move down to his still hard cock and suck her juices off. She slides on top of him and rubs her pussy over his thickness.

He speaks, saying, "Turn around, and get on your knees." She complies but she recognizes that voice as the bald, muscular man from the bar... Before she can think more of the situation, he rams his cock deep into her asshole. She cries out, first in pain but then in pure pleasure. He pounds deep into her ass showing no mercy. Once again, she finds her clit and begins rubbing it furiously. Aching for him to pound it harder, she begs, "Please fuck my ass! Fuck it harder!" His nails dig into her ass as he slams her closer to him. He lets out a deep moan of his own, and she feels that cock throbbing inside her ass and the hot load squirting deep inside her hole drives her to another orgasm. The lights turn on, and there are four other men in the room, all attractive. The one that has the smaller cock walks over to her and begins sucking her pussy and ass, sucking out every drop of cum and her juices that he can. Afterwards, he gets up and the others follow him out of the room. She looks behind her and directly into the man's eyes from the bar. Her face red with shame, he throws her clothing to her, and tells her to get dressed. She complies and begins slipping her panties on quickly and slips her dress over her head.

He walks towards the open door, and she follows, realizing she was in a basement. He leads her out the front door and into his car. They drive silently back toward the bar. He stops the car, looks over, and tells her to get out. Ashlee opens the door and gives him one last look, longingly staring towards his groin/ She gets out quickly and shuts the door. As she walks back into the bar, she says to herself, *I should definitely come to this bar more often.*

Natalie's First Bukakke Gangbang: An Erotic Gangbang, Bukakke, and Creampie Story

"Would you like a refill?" The waitress asked; as if it was even a serious question. It had always bothered Natalie when wait staff had to ask if she wanted more to drink even as they served her food.

"Please" she replied with a smile, though her eyes gave away its lack of authenticity. How else, she wondered, was she expected to quench her thirst? Let alone the fact the plush price she willingly paid day in and day out for the carbonated beverage; she wanted her money's worth. Even since moving to the big city, Natalie had never gotten into the coffee scene. With a Starbucks on every corner, it seemed an uphill battle to find a large, fresh fountain soda that had that extra bite to it the store bought equivalent never quite was able to match. At least she didn't call it 'pop' anymore; her Midwest upbringing wasn't a talking point she particularly liked to associate with. No, Natalie was a sophisticated lady now. That's what she kept telling herself, and after three grueling years of groveling for minimum wage day after day to escape her small town upbringing it felt deserved.

As she sat alone at her table pondering her life since moving to the city, she gazed out the restaurant window onto the dusk-lit street, street lamps flickering on one-by-one. It was a beautiful evening and the temperature was just right. "Maybe I'll go for a walk later," she thought to herself as she bit down on a sensual strip steak. Nothing paired better with her ice-cold soda like the taste of meat in her mouth. Halfway through her meal she noticed a man at the bar glancing her direction. But he wasn't looking at her, was he? Natalie was a thin, attractive lady and she knew it, but had found in recent days she wasn't the best big city flirt. Her typical witty, warm sense humor she used at home didn't represent the elegant woman she wanted to be. Slowly, Natalie stroked her dark brown hair over her ear and the edge of her mouth curved ever so slightly into a smile. Crossing her legs in her short black dress, she glanced every so gracefully at the bar. Not a stare, but long enough to suggest it wasn't accidental. As she looked she saw the man smirk as he slowly sipped his drink in the company of a friend. Pleased with her successful first impression, she resumed eating her meal and figured her encounter with the stranger was complete, like an exchange with a cashier at the local convenience store when buying a pop.

As she resumed her imaginative looks out into the darkening scenery she now called home, she couldn't help but feel elated as the caffeine coursed through her veins. As she finished her meal, and motioned for the check, Natalie yawned slightly as she remembered the long walk home.

"Tired?" a deep voice implored. Startled, Natalie quickly turned around to see the man from the bar stroll around her chair and stop, hands resting on the chair next to her. Realizing her silence "oh, no, not really, I mean, yes, but…" she stammered, her mind barely catching back up to the present from the inner recesses of her imagination. The man smiled, showing his beautifully white teeth, and asked "is this seat taken?"

Flush red, Natalie looked down to compose herself while letting out a small laugh. Looking back up with a soft smile, "Please," she responded motioning towards the chair.

"I couldn't help but notice a beautiful woman sitting all alone on a Friday night and had to intervene," he said in a smooth masculine tone.

"My white knight?" she retorted with a smile. "I was actually supposed to meet someone for dinner, but he never showed." It was a lie, and she knew it, but didn't want to seem alone. On second thought, which was worse? Eating alone or being stood up? Either way there was a handsome man, thick brown hair and a sexy five o'clock shadow, sitting across from her now.

"Well it is a good thing I came over then, isn't it?" he countered, leaning in. "I'm John, and my friend over there is Tim." Natalie glanced over at the bar and saw a man leaning his back against it, who waved. She waved back and looked back at John. "I'm Natalie, it's nice to meet you," she said as her hand jerked forward uncontrollably fast to greet the stranger.

John smiled, like a child holding an adorable puppy for the first time, and grabbed her hand. If Natalie could have been any redder in the face, she probably would have died from embarrassment, but those feelings quickly subsided as he slowly lifted her hand and kissed the back of it, never breaking eye contact. He slowly returned her hand to the table and said through his heartening smile ",It's nice to meet you." As the words came out of his mouth Natalie's heart melted, how could she ever say no to that face? "My friend and I were wondering if you wanted to come back to our place for drinks," he added. "It's not far from here if you're interested."

"Sure!" she exclaimed. She wasn't typically an impulsive person, but something seemed different about this man. What did she have to lose, she thought. As she left the restaurant and walked down the street the man slowly put his hand around her waist as his friend trolled a few yards ahead of them. The smell of the fresh air brought a smile to her face, as if each breath she took was a gift as it filled her lungs. The tree lined streets casted elegant shadows on passing cars as the city bustled around them. A few minutes and some light exchanges later…

"We're here," John said as he motioned toward some stairs leading down. It led to an old split-level basement entrance. The building was red brick, sandwiched between identical buildings. As she took the hand he offered down the narrow steps, a cold breeze blew through Natalie's hair such that small Goosebumps rose on the back of her neck. "Welcome to our humble abode" John exclaimed as the other man unlocked the door and entered the apartment. "Can I get you something to drink?" He asked.

"Rum and diet?" she implored.

"Coming right up." John replied. "Feel free to sit wherever you like."

Natalie slowly looked around as the roommate nonchalantly returned the deadbolt into its original position and sauntered over to the armchair. The apartment was dimly lit, but still cozy. It wasn't as luxurious as John's clothing suggested his lifestyle entailed, but then again rent was through the roof in this part of the city. The kitchen was just off to the right through an open doorway from the living room in which she stood. The frayed carpet on the floor was offset by large black leather furniture throughout the room. She strolled to the nearest couch and sat down, absorbed into the plush cushioning. John returned after a few minutes and handed her a drink, clutching a beer of his own. As they talked and generally enjoyed themselves, she began to feel elated, and fluttery. John was a businessman that worked downtown, black suit type of guy; she liked that. As he took off his jacket she noticed his bulging arms through his tight undershirt. Natalie's heart swooned. They talked about everything and anything for a good long while as she sipped her sweat drink. The smooth cola flowed down her throat as John talked. Long enough for a second drink, in fact. She didn't know what it was exactly about him, but she could feel the word yes on the tip of her tongue as if she would do anything he asked. Pausing for a moment, it was obvious John could tell, and he liked it.

With a sharp glint in his eye, he casually put his hand on her knee and began rubbing his thumb back and forth slower than a turtle walking. She looked down, heart racing, and back into his soft gaze. Natalie felt good. No, she felt great - better than she had in months. They sat there silent for what seemed like minutes as his thumb slowly began to move faster and faster back and forth. Her soft silk dress was the perfect rubbing material, but his persistence began to warm things up.

"So…" she said motioning her head towards his friend. She had forgotten he was there, the quiet man he was.

"He doesn't mind" John whispered as he began sliding his hand up her tight thigh. Natalie's mind was racing, his strong hands caressing her leg was making her crazy. She could hardly think of anything to say. That or she just didn't care anymore.

"If you.. uh.. say so" she stammered in pleasure as she slowly laid back onto the couch. John smirked as he slowly climbed on top of her, hand by hand like a lion in the savanna hunting its prey. As he climbed he slowly kissed her stomach inch by inch, pausing between each kiss as Natalie sighed in pleasure from the touch of his lips. Natalie didn't know what to do with her hands, but fortunately they had a mind of their own. As he climbed she caressed his strong shoulders and squeezed at every kiss. She couldn't help it anymore. As he arrived, to her breasts her left hand slowly slid down to her inner thigh and began rubbing herself through the dress. Everything felt amazing, like nothing she had ever experienced before. The only thing she could concentrate on was John. Clutching her breasts in both hands as he lay inches above her face with his weight on his knees and elbows, he paused above her mouth and grinned.

"You like this, don't you?" he asked. She nodded and let out a small laugh as her busy hands relaxed and lay in anticipation. Hands attached to her breasts, even with his large hands, he could barely get a majority hold on each - which made them even better to rub. Through her bra he could probably see how hard her nipples had gotten from the intense rubbing, but, like everything else, paid it no attention. John's deep voice was all that mattered to her.

"You want him to watch, don't you?" he enquired looking over, matching his friend's devious gaze. Again she nodded, not saying a word. If John wanted it, the good Midwestern girl inside her was obligated to oblige. Or was it something else. "Say it" he retorted.

"I want him to watch," she said as she grinned widely, her hands grasping his waist and pulling him closer. Even through his tight pants she could feel the large present he had for her.

"You like any audience, I can tell. You want a bigger one; how about we invite some of the neighbors over? I'll get you an audience, just like you'll like." He said in a matter of fact tone brushing the hair to the side in a loving motion. Natalie tried to think about it, there was something inside her that was trying to say something, but she couldn't think. Yes. That is all she could think, over and over again. She nodded. Everything felt right, even if it was wrong. All she could think about was being pleasured. He nodded to his friend who pulled out his phone and returned to the helpless girl yearning for him inches away. Lowering his face until his lips brushed the soft tender outlines of her mouth. She could feel his breath brushing across her cheek as her hands pulled him tighter, closer, until she couldn't bear it anymore! The passion in which she kissed him would put some Shakespearean poetry to shame. Like a million fireworks going off, his lips gave her all the satisfaction she desired. Energy swelled through her flowing down from her neck through her breasts and stomach to her legs. Every inch of her body convulsed towards John's rock hard body trying to get closer. She felt as if she could never get close enough as their hips seesawed back and forth. A moment later the front door was unlocked and a man came in.

She hadn't thought about it, but he must have had a key. All she could think about was John. Nothing in the world mattered right now. After a few minutes of passionate embrace the room was full of men shrouded in the outskirts of the room and the door re-locked. Their whispers were inaudible, but their presence gave the room a new excited vibe. John stopped, with his forehead pressing on hers; she could feel him pressing his hard cock against her dress as his heavy breath filled the room like a dog in heat.

"Tonight," he gasped, exhausted from her enthusiasm, "we have a very special gift for you Natalie. One you won't soon forget. Something just for you, and no one else." Pushing off he looked down at her as he kneeled on the couch, still straddling her wide hips. "I told you I'd get an audience." He proclaimed, swinging an arm open to show off their new guests Natalie broke her gaze and looked over at the men shrouded across the room. The lights were dimmer than before, but there were spotlight cans above the couch pointing down on her. There was no artwork on the wall, but she could see the dim outline of a previous owner's piece. Natalie was the art now, though. Natalie was the star in this production. The men all stared, beer in some hands, dark glasses and hats on others. She could not see well, but it looked like most were touching themselves through their pants. She liked that.

"Do it!" one shouted.

"Yeah!" the others cried.

"Take it off." John looked down at Natalie and smiled. The same smile he made when he first sat down with her at a restraint, a distant memory. It was the smile she would say yes to anything for. And as he smiled he crossed his arms and grabbed the bottom of his shirt, lifting it above his head. He had a black tribal tattoo strewn across his shoulder all the way across his huge pecs. She knew he was fit, but his blaringly obvious abdominals told an even better story.

"Turn over" he ordered, and Natalie obliged. He pressed his pelvis against her ass and began slowly gyrating his hips. As he did so, supporting himself with his left hand, he slowly unzipped that sexy, silk, black dress. Natalie began moaning imagining him penetrating her however he wanted. Soon enough he had both her arms out of her dress and turned her back over.

"Let me help you out of this," John pressed. "Your crowd wants to see." And of course Natalie obliged. As he slowly slipped her dress off her, lifting her at the waist so she didn't have to lift a finger, she began to feel the full force of the lights above her on her perfectly tanned skin. Her healthy glow shone bright as if she was on a sunny beach in the spring, and she could just lay there and relax all day long.

Returning her gaze to John, she looked at him, bending her knees and sliding her right hand between her legs and asked, "Can you give it to me? Please? I need it." Dropping her dress to the ground John pressed against her, again, but this time much harder. Returning to his elbows they began the dance of lips again and continued to press closer and closer together. John suddenly pulled to the side and kissed her cheek, then her jaw, and then her neck. Natalie screamed in pleasure! She had no mind for the lights, or the crowd again, she just wanted John. Turning to their sides he slipped his arms around her to undo her fitting silk black bra that had an elegant white lace on its border, her large breasts begging to be released from their captor. Like an expert, John pried the clasps apart with ease and slowly removed the bra arm by arm, her back to the audience as if to build suspense. A few had unzipped their pants now, hands down their boxers. Their excitement was obvious, with small grunts of approval as their entertainers performed. Flipping her back on her back Natalie's breasts bounced wildly from left to right as they returned to their natural resting place. John saw this, and became visually excited as he quickly descended to meet them.

Flicking his tongue lightly over her exposed breast he then cupped a nipple with his mouth and began sucking. From within he nibbled ever so gently as Natalie screamed even louder in pleasure. She was the art and he was the artist, an expert at his trade. Both hands clasping her freed breasts he looked her in the eye as he continued to play with her nipples. The excitement was palpable. He had saturated her breasts with sensory information she almost couldn't process. Every touch, titillation and bite brought her to heights she had never experience and just couldn't get enough of it. As the pace slowed to a more intimate rhythm, John's hands once again returned to her waistline as he kissed his way slowly to her stomach.

As he removed the tight G-string panties separating him from the most perfectly pink pussy he had ever seen, he continued kissing around the side of her inner thigh. Wet, succulent brushes with his lips. The men held their breath as she became truly exposed. Many of their rock hard dicks being flung out left and right from the shadows of their boxers. Some had even taken off their shirt, or pulled it around their head to expose tender nipples to play with. Either way, the sound of their long strokes excited Natalie even more as she looked over and smiled. Something about the lights and the theatrics of it all made her want to give them an amazing show, give them pleasure, give them whatever they wanted. The last string of her pant-ies departed her toes as John dropped them to the floor to join her silky black dress, he returned to her pink pussy. Completely shaved his tongue was eagerly met by the invitingly moist pussy. He started by lightly liking the top of her pussy's tight lips, and slowly went a little deeper. As if to keep her on edge, he occasionally did a full mouth kiss, or went deeper before returning to the edge. Natalie moaned, again and again and his tongue brushed passed the clit, teasing it. She wanted to touch herself, make it feel even better, but she waited be-cause John was enjoying it. The crowd was enjoying it. As he worked her pussy with his wet tongue, she began to relax some as her lips opened to greet each pass.

His rhythm picked up until he was almost tongue fucking her tight pussy. Her moans grew louder and louder as she lounged for his attention to turn to her clit. It was delicate, but she was ready. She ran her hand through his thick brown hair as he dug deeper and deeper, his lips separating hers. With one long and delicate tongue stroke John journeyed up to her clit and began slowly massaging. It was like liking a small pearl; he knew exactly where she wanted it. Her hips began to rise as her moans filled the room. "Oh, yeah!" She exclaimed. The men in the room were now stroking their hard cocks, as if they were getting ready for something, many fixating on Natalie's supple breasts as they jiggled to John's rhythm wanting a touch. John then ascended, kissing her stomach and returning to her mouth.

"You like that, don't you. I bet you'd like a hard cock in your pussy now, wouldn't you?" he sneered. Natalie Nodded. John stood up and began undoing his belt and pants. As he slid off his pants, he gripped a huge cock through his loose boxers. "You want this, don't you?" he stated. It was at least nine inches and thick too. Natalie had never seen a cock that big and was dying to try it. Every ounce in her body wanted it inside of her. He slowly slipped his huge dick over the elastic band and slapped it against his hand. Natalie stood up on one elbow, barely able to think of anything but his cock in her mouth as he pressed forward. His thick cock slid slowly into her small mouth - so far that her cheek protruded and she gagged a little. John liked that.

"Get on your knees so your audience can see you," he ordered. She did so. John grabbed the back of her head with one hand as he put his other hand behind him, twisting his torso towards the crowd. He forced her head down on his thick cock as he pressed forward with his hips. He let out a moan as she grabbed his exposed shaft and began using it to jack him off. Now it was her turn to use her tongue. She continued to suck him longer than she thought possible, her jaw throbbing from the act, but she continued until he pulled her up enjoying the experience too much to stop. As he pulled her off, his thick cock bounced down dripping with her saliva.

Without a word he sat her on the table, and bent her down. John's friend pushed the magazines and other adornments off the table to make room. As Natalie lay back, letting her thick brown hair flow back behind her hair, waving it as she went, John got down on his knees. The table wasn't very high, but it was the perfect height to align her tight pink pussy with his throbbing cock. Natalie was begging for it. John's dick was begging for it. Everyone it the room was begging for it - with hardly any clothes left. Slowly, John slipped his primed dick into her wet pussy. At first he played with it a little, slapping his dick down on it and putting just the tip in. He stared at Natalie as he had one hand on his cock, and one on her right breast. He wanted to see her anguish as he put his monstrous cock into her. Inch by inch, Natalie moaned in pleasure and pain. She loved the pain, it made her feel alive. She felt so gifted to be receiving such an amazing cock. She didn't want anything else. She could feel every part of his cock move slowly into her as the walls of her vagina pressed in ever so tightly. As his dick nearly disappeared into the pink palace, John let out a moan as he exclaimed, "You're so tight!"

"Just for you," she responded.

Leaning over, "Just for me?" he said with a smile as he went the last inch. Natalie lifted her neck, wide-eyed with her mouth gaping open. She had lost her breath from the experience. Then, suddenly, returning it down and letting out a long, well deserved oh in immense pleasure from his long, thick cock reaching into the inner recesses of her pussy. Pleased, John began fucking her tight pussy as he grabbed her bouncing breasts as handholds. Their rhythm picked up as the moans once again filled the room. The crowd watched as John's thick, throbbing cock repeatedly entered and slid out of her pussy with every exit stretching out appearing as if it was pulling it back in. A minute later one of the men stepped forward and put a hand on John's shoulder. "Let me in," he ordered in a rough biker's voice. John looked up and smiled, pulling out. Natalie smiled at the amazing feeling of Johns cock even after he had exited. She slid her hand down to her clit as she waited to be entered again. This time the man grabbed her legs by the ankles and spread her wide. His cock was an average length, but thicker than most cucumbers, veins popping out from all sides! He spit on his dick, letting it slowly reach down and drop onto his ridiculously thick cock as he slowly slid it into her primed pussy.

While she had barely taken John's massive cock, nothing could have prepared her for this. The man wasted no time waiting for her comfort as he pushed in. Natalie's breath increased as water filled her eyes. Her mind seared with pain but it soon dissipated as he began pounding his dick into her. A few tears trickled from her eyes and she moaned. Everyone in the room smiled. The feeling of being their star returned to Natalie as she began staring at the man pleasuring her.

"Harder" she demanded, "fuck me harder!" The man gave a deep laugh as he pushed in like a jackhammer. Natalie's head swung back as she screamed in pleasure and pain. She felt like she was a part of the world, and knew what it meant to be alive at that moment. What she was experiencing was the only thing that mattered, and she was so lucky to get this huge throbbing cock inside of her. Her pussy pulled harder and harder every time his cock exited as his veins created the perfect surface to massage every part of her vagina. Man after man, hard cock after hard cock, they each took turns pounding to no resolve and forcing their massive cocks down her throat. Natalie loved every second of it. Everything just seemed right. Her favorite was the man with the curved dick; something about it hit her in all the right spots and made her scream louder than any of the rest. Eventually she began to get close to climaxing. John, who had been sitting on the couch touching himself for most of the festivities, noticed her change in breath. He stood up, excited, eyes beaming at all the men. "She's ready!" he roared.

As if a preconceived signal, the men pulled out, cocks dripping, and began stroking above her. Those sitting down, or towards the wall began to huddle around her. Their strokes became louder and louder as John knelt down at the foot of the table to resume his rightful place. This made Natalie very happy. She didn't want to give her precious orgasm to anyone else. As he began thrusting into her now looser, but still tight pussy, the men groaned - including John. Suddenly, one man pushed past all the rest as he let out exhausted breaths rising in pitch. His hand speed up wrapped around his long cock as his breaths hastened and his entire body tensed up. Finally he let out a huge high pitch sigh has his cock spasmed shooting a huge stream of white semen on Natalie's stomach. Then another. His body relaxed as he began to breathe deeply. The men laugh and made the sounds of approval as the man slunk back through the ranks. Other men began shooting off all over Natalie but all she could think about was John's thick. Long. Throbbing cock pounding her faster than before. In and out, in and out, he sped up. It was John's turn to begin to tense up, holding his breath and breathing erratically. Natalie followed suit as her legs began pressing in on John's chiseled body. His thrusts became less abdominal bends and more full body lunges forward into the depths of her pussy. It was as if he couldn't get as deep as he wanted. Pounding harder and harder, John's eyebrows raised as his jaw dropped. Slowly, he began to breathe a little, and then more, as he continued to pound her tight pink pussy. He then let out a long moan as his head tilted back looking towards the ceiling in intense pleasure. Natalie was almost there, but she could feel a thick load being unleashed inside of her.

That did it for her, she was there. Her legs squeezed around John's body and pulled him inside of her as his mouth opened moaning loudly. She relaxed, attempting to catch her breath as the men finished around her. One by one they released their loads all over her body and face and slunk away. John soon pulled out, and Natalie let out a final moan. She could feel John's warm load in the lips of her pussy, and she smiled. As she sat there, covered in a warm sea of jizz, she looked at John standing above her - that same smile she loved.

He lifted her up, and carried her to another room to clean her up. She had not realized it, but she had grown very tired. As he wiped her thin, toned body off with a warm towel, and pulled the covers over her exposed breasts, he kissed her forehead. "You did good," John said in a soft tone. He then set a cold unopened can of coke on the bedside table as he left, "My little girl did good."

Gangbanged by Four Hindu Priests at Temple

(as retold by Hannah Butler)

Hello, my name is Anjali. I was born in a very traditional family in India. Unfortunately, sexual freedom for a girl in India is very restricted. So, when I turned 18, I got hooked to my own fantasy world. Just like other girls of my age, I used to be very hot and sexy. Well, I am still very sexy and young girl of 22 years of age, but at that age my pussy used to be wet all the time. Sometimes, I had to use pads to avoid the sticky feeling in my panties. I don't know about other girls, but I always desired to fuck three or four boys of my class. In fact, I was getting very desperate to see and feel a man's "lund" (dick). Whenever I was in close proximity of handsome boys or even middle-aged men, my dripping pussy lips used to open and close from unusual excitement. Somehow, I used to control my sexual thoughts during the day, but there was no respite in the nights.

During the nights, my hips used to jerk at regular intervals and a stream of pussy juices used to wet the crack of my ass. I couldn't sleep without inserting a finger in my pussy and dreaming about my classmates while masturbating. I had to masturbate three or four times a night. For almost two years (from the age of 18 to 20), my sexual life was limited to fingering and masturbating while dreaming as if my classmates were fucking me. Despite my intense desire to be fucked by strong men, I was very timid and shy in approaching any prospective mate. However, my first sexual encountered with a man took place when I was 18 years of age.

By the time I turned 18, my boobs had developed to their full potential because I used to fondle them while masturbating. My young figure with well-shaped tits and ass attracted many boys and men. In fact, they wanted to fuck me, but I was very shy in approaching them or giving them a go ahead signal. I just wanted them to take charge and dominate my body without any signal or hint on my part. I have some idea about sexually attracting handsome men and exciting them until they lose control, but held back. Luckily, my first sexual encounter with a man occurred without the need to do anything special. My sexy body and perky boobs did all the work for me. I would love to believe that my ample bosom grabbed men's attention, and all of them desired to touch them or take them in their hungry mouths.

On a train, travelling with my parents to attend a marriage ceremony, I finally got my first taste of lund. We had reserved our place in the sleeping coach and I insisted on sleeping on the side room because I was wondering the possibility of masturbating in the night. I was aware that it may not be possible to masturbate for two or three days due to lack of privacy at the relative's place. Incidentally, a middle-aged gentleman requested the permission of my parents to stand there as he boarded the train at the last minute. In India, trains are very crowded and people even travel in the reserved sleeping coaches at times. Considering his gentle personality, my parents allowed him to stand there. I was disappointed as he was standing nearby and there was no chance of masturbating under the sheet.

After a few hours, everybody started sleeping, but I was very desperate to masturbate. It was not possible to go to sleep without relieving my sexual tension. Just like other nights, a tiny stream of pussy juices made my pussy wet and ran through the crack of my ass. Although, my sexy body was fully covered under the sheet, I was very hesitant to masturbate in the presence of a stranger, but my pussy was not listening to any logic. It had become such a ritual that my body could not be controlled. My hips started automatically jerking at regular intervals. My mind was full of sexy thoughts and I started dreaming about my classmates once again. Suddenly I felt a rough hand on my lower abdomen. My hips jerked violently and I shivered as if a bolt of lightning had struck me. My heart's pounding increased as he started slowly moving his hands over my body, rubbing around my thighs, stomach, and the bulging mound of my pussy. I realized that the gentleman lost his control and started feeling my body over the sheet. I was totally numbed by the spontaneous sexual response from my body. A big gush of pussy juices made my panties soaking wet and my legs were automatically spread wide as he proceeded towards my pussy. I was experiencing a sexual ecstasy because such a satisfying excitement had never happened while I fingered my pussy. My approval encouraged him and he began rubbing over my pussy. Realizing my wetness over the sheet, he made his way under the sheet and opened the strings of my nightwear. The touch of his rough hands made me almost intoxicated with lust. He lowered my garb and slipped his hand through the side of my panties. The moment he touched my pussy lips, they responded with spontaneous pulsations and a very powerful orgasm rocked my brain, my body, and made it difficult to remain quiet. I had never reached such a frenzy orgasm while fingering myself, and so my pussy juices made his fingers very, very slippery. He started rubbing my pussy lips, ass crack, and clit. My entire pussy area became a flooded mess. Realizing his full control over my body, his other hand started feeling and folding my boobs one by one. He removed the sheet from my boobs and tried to remove my top, but couldn't succeed as I was wearing a very tight suit. So, he couldn't directly touch my boobs. I wished he could have gained direct access to my boobs by unzipping my back side, but he had no idea about it. He decided to press and pinch my nipples over the suit. His tingling fingers right over my pussy lips and clit made me so crazy that I enjoyed a very satisfying boob massage over my suit. After playing with my pussy and boobs for some time, he inserted his middle finger inside my pussy and started fingering me. He was very expert in fingering pussy and rubbing the clit. I reached my second orgasm in no time. My pussy was filled with fresh juices and it started making sound while he fingered. Luckily, the sound of finger fucking was lost in the noise of the speeding train. Under this intoxication of mindless lust, I wished to touch his dick. In fact, I wanted to touch and feel a dick even before I started inserting fingers in my pussy.

Unfortunately, he did nothing to let me or force me to touch or lick his dick. He just enjoyed fingering my pussy and made me cum four times. So, I decided to give my response and removed his hands from my pussy, fixed my clothes, and went to the toilet. I thought that he would follow me and give me the chance to take his dick. I waited for some time, but the bastard never showed up. I should have told him to follow. Anyway, I cleaned up my mess and retuned to find that the man had gone.

From this incident, the stranger dominated my sexual fantasy. The imagination of this incident fueled my fingering episodes for the next two years before I decided to seduce men and enjoy real sex with them.

Although, I shared a few nights with my close friend Anita, by licking pussies or using thick candles as dildos to ravage each other's pussy, this seemed less exciting in comparison to the chance of having straight sex with middle-aged men. Yes, I am more inclined to middle-aged men as my friend told me that mature men don't create any emotional problems in life. So, when I reached 20 years of age without taking any dicks into my virginal pussy, I planned to seduce men, but the concerns of privacy and lack of a secure place proved the greatest hurdles in my adventure.

However, if girls want a dick in their pussy, they can find several ways because dicks are always searching for beautiful and tight pussies. There is no lack of dick in the world. I found my redemption from sexual restriction at a temple. Yes, one day I noticed that a handsome priest, perhaps in his late thirties, was ogling at my boobs. Realizing that nobody would ever stop me from regularly visiting the temple, I decided my best plan was to seduce the priest.

So I started visiting the temple in sexy outfits, making my boobs, curvy figure, and ass even more tantalizing than ever. Very soon, I started realizing that all the four priests at the temple gave me special attention. It was so amusing that my perky tits and well-shaped ass was giving them an instant hard on. I started talking to the priest and seduced him by occasionally showing my round ass under the pretext of picking up some intentionally dropped objects. On some occasions, I went to temple without wearing any bra and showed him my bouncing boobs. Several days passed but nothing happened, and I started working on a new plan to have fun with my servant by lifting my skirt and showing him a clean view of my pussy while pretending to sleep.

So, one day I pulled up my skirt just before he was supposed to enter the room for house cleaning. The trick worked and he slowly lifted my skirt even higher to look at my pussy. As I wasn't wearing any panty, he got a clear look of my clean and wet pussy. He kept on looking at it, but somebody called him and he quickly left my room. Now, it became a routine for him to sneak into my room and watch my wet pussy by slowly lifting my night gown. After a few days, he developed the courage to touch and feel my pussy and pampered by my soft moaning, he even started licking my pussy. I entered a new phase of enjoyment as his licking always gave me an exploding orgasm in the morning. Unfortunately, he was not supposed to spend more time in my room, and I was still undecided whether I should let my servant fuck me.

After a month, I went to the temple during the festivals. The priests seemed really excited to see me. One of them came to me and asked for my help in some preparations. I followed him to the temple basement where one girl, clearly just eighteen, was already preparing the offerings to the deity. She was even sexier looking than I am. Her boobs were bigger than mine and her ass was a pure delight for any man. We started working together and after finishing the preparations, she offered me a drink. Within a few minutes of drinking it, I felt extremely sleepy.

When I regained my senses, I found myself tied to the bed in a small room. My clothes were removed and I was lying there completely naked. Three priests were busy in enjoying my luscious body. Two of them were playing with my boobs and licking and sucking my nipples. One of them was licking my pussy. My young body had already responded to their licking and nibbling. My hip was gyrating with each movement of his tongue. The fourth priest was standing there naked, slowly stroking his dick. His black dick was thick and huge. My years of dreaming had finally started to come true but I was very frightened to see the huge dicks of four strong priests. However, the fear quickly turned into excitement and ecstasy as I reached my orgasm. My whole body wriggled and I exploded with a very loud moan. The head priests smiled and ordered others to stand beside the bed. He came over me, smeared his dick with my pussy juices and started rubbing his dick over my clitoris. It was the first dick that had ever touched my pussy. I was breathing heavily in expectation of engulfing the whole dick inside my pussy, but he ordered me to request for fucking.

He said, "Request me, and say please fuck me." I kept quiet. I wanted his dick inside me, but I was not willing to say so. My silence enraged him and he started slapping my boobs. The rubbing his dick even more aggressively on my pussy lips and slapping on my boob made me moan with each hit. The other priests were getting restless. One of them was really excited to see my black nipples and brown circles around them. He requested the head priest to let him suck my nipples and make me excited enough to request. In fact, the dick of all the three priests had become so stiff that they were feeling uncomfortable. They wanted the head priests to fuck me so that they can quickly fuck me in turns. Rather than requesting them to fuck me, I started moaning in a very sensuous tone. My sensuous moaning, luscious body, and the irresistible smell from the young pussy made it impossible for the head priest to hold out any longer. He entered my pussy and started fucking me as if he never had any girl in his whole life. By this time, my pussy had become so wet and I was so excited that his huge dick easily rolled in and out of my pussy. The experience of a dick in my pussy was totally different than condom fitted candles. It was hot and throbbing. Each thrust of his dick prompted me to respond and I lifted my hips to match his onslaught. Within a few minutes, the head priest came inside my pussy. His warm sperm felt like a godly treasure inside my pussy. He stood up and left me to the mercy of the other three priests. They wasted no time in licking off the sperm laden juices from my pussy. One of the priests untied my hands and ordered me to get on all fours and take his dick. He fucked me doggy style. They took turns to fuck me in every possible poses. It was the most wonderful day of my life. I realized that the pussy of a girl is a virtual doorway to heaven. I was in heaven for almost five hours. When I felt pain on my pussy mound due to a very rigorous fucking episode, I requested them let me ride their healthy cocks. I told that I will regularly visit to enjoy fun and adventure in my life. They tied me to the bed and retuned with the girl who had drugged me.

They started ripping her clothes. The girl smiled at me and bent over the bed post. One of the priests started fucking her from behind. Her big boobs bounced with each thrust and she started moaning like a professional whore. Her moaning and crying made them insatiable and they took turns to fuck her for another three hours. After filling her pussy with their sperms and shooting some of their loads on my boobs, they said that we could go home. Since that day, I discovered my sexual freedom. Now, I have become more open to men and have learned to invite them by winking and even grabbing their dicks in public.

Orgy on Bourbon Street:
Sarah's First Taste of Pussy and Getting Gang-banged by Cops

Sarah was fresh out of college, and taking a long deserved break from all the years she spent studying. She decided that she would go to New Orleans and spend a few weeks taking in the culture and the wonderful food. She started out on Bourbon street as most tourists do. The smells were rather conflicting to her. She could smell alcohol, vomit, and amazing foods, and urine. It was a heady concoction, and she decided that she had better get a drink soon. It was a Thursday night in the Quarter, and there was plenty of action.

She went into the first bar that seemed to be hopping, and soon found out why. There were half naked women everywhere… she even saw a young college girl sucking a cock while the recipient was sitting at the bar. She was not sure this was quite the place for her, but she decided "What the hell, I am out for a good time, and I want to experience new things."

She went to the bar, ordered a hurricane, and began sipping it. As she looked around the bar, she began to notice that there was more blatant sexual activity going on… she also noticed that her panties were beginning to get damp. As the night moved on, she drank more, and begin to mingle. She actually sat down at a table where there were two girls eating each other's pussies right on the table. She was surprised to find herself stroking the inner thigh of one of the girls. The girl responded by leaning over and deep kissing Sarah, something Sarah had never experienced. She found that it was not unpleasant, and began to probe her tongue deeper and more passionately into her new found friend's mouth.

Before she knew it, her fingers were moist and warm as she let them slide into the other girl's wet pussy. Just as she began to rub her own pussy, the worst happened. The cops showed up. They were none too happy, either. Everyone, including Sarah, who was involved in fucking, sucking, or licking, was rounded up, and taken to a back room. There was about 30 people, men and women alike. The cops began telling how it was illegal to have sex in public in New Orleans, but maybe they could work something out... Some of the people chuckled. This seems to be exactly what normally happens around here on a regular basis. Sarah was scared shitless. One cop in particular, seemed to show an interest in Sarah and her friends.

He walked right up to Sarah and stuck his hand right under her skirt. Much to her surprise, she was rather turned on by this. He grabbed her friends left tit with his other hand. Sarah began to rub his cock through his uniform with one hand while rubbing her new found female friends bare pussy with her other. At first she was going along because she thought it would keep her out of jail, but now she was just horny as hell and ready to fuck. The four of them were all over each other. There were two mouths, hungrily sucking the cops cock, and the third girl was licking the asses and pussies of Sarah and the other girl. Sarah had never been fucked in her ass with a tongue before, but she would be from now on! She didn't know such a thing could be so pleasurable. She was learning all sorts of new things about herself.

Then, without any warning, another cop came up behind Sarah. Thankfully, her pussy was sopping wet, because he rammed his hard, throbbing cock right up her cunt from behind while she was still sharing the first cops cock with her friend. One after another, the cops would randomly come up, fucking different girls for a while. She finally got to fuck the cop that she had been sucking. She really liked the way he felt, both in her mouth, and in her pussy. He laid her on a table, she spread her legs wide and high. He entered her slowly... agonizingly slowly. She wanted to feel the full length of his cock as deep as possible. Finally, she did. He thrust that last inch in so fast that she came immediately. She yelped, she writhed, she moaned, she cried. It was a short orgasm, but very intense. It was not the first of the night, nor would it be the last. As he got into a rhythm, pumping her cunt and pinching her nipples, a new girl came up and began to lick her clit. She hadn't realized before tonight just how much she liked women. She never even considered herself bi-curious, but she was certain that she was more than curious now... she KNEW that she wanted to taste a sweet pussy for herself. About the time of that realization, the cop suddenly pulled his cock out of her pussy and moved towards her head. The girl moved right in, continuing to eat her pussy, and sticking her wonderful tongue deep inside her cunt. The cop thrust his cock in Sarah's mouth and she began to suck furiously. It only took a few seconds, and she felt his warm, sticky cum flow down the back of her throat. As she felt it, she could not contain herself, and she began to cum, actually squirting on the girl between her legs. This was the most intense orgasm she had ever experienced! It was like none other. At first, once she stopped coming, she was embarrassed. She had never heard of a woman doing that before. But the girl between her legs didn't stop licking, so she figured it must be ok.

The cop left, without a word, and moved into the crowd. Sarah decided to take the opportunity to switch places with the girls that she had just soaked with her last orgasm. It was time for Sarah to finally get her first taste of pussy. She tentatively licked this girls wet bald pussy. She found that it tasted marvelous. The young lady certainly responded well to Sarah's tongue. She was not certain what to do, but decided to try to imitate what some of the guys in college had done to her that felt good. It seemed to be working, as the more she did, the more the young lady writhed around on the table. After eating her first pussy for a good ten minutes, she noticed a couple of girls grinding their pussies together… it looked like they were fucking, but their clits were just rubbing together. Sarah knew that she had to try that. She found a more comfortable spot for her and her first lesbian lover, and she laid her down, then positioned herself, intertwining her legs with her friends. Then, slowly, she began grinding her wet pussy against her friend's wet pussy. Their juices were combining, and the more she ground, the more wet they got. She played with one of her erect nipples and one of her lovers erect nipples. All the while, she was grinding away. As her friend began cumming, she realized that she was about to explode too. They both came explosively. They were both squirting on each other, and now she realized how enjoyable that was too. The crowd was beginning to thin out. Sarah had completely forgotten that they were supposedly in trouble for public lewdness. She realized that they were free to go. She was thankful that she was not being taken to jail, but she was more thankful that her eyes had been opened to what a sexual creature she truly was. There was so much more to sex than she had previously experienced, and New Orleans seemed to be a great place to explore her sexuality. She thought to herself, that she might just have to stay a while in the Big Easy... Yes, she certainly could not wait to go out tomorrow night. She was certain that it would be an eventful night!

Carnival Rides:
Gangbanged by the Trapeze Trio and Face Riding a Lesbian in the Parking Lot

As she walked past the tent where a trio of trapeze artists had been performing Carla hesitated before finally arriving at her desired spot. She honestly did not think that anyone would respond to the haphazardly written ad she'd scrawled on a napkin and posted on the muddied fence next to the carnival's restroom area. The restroom area was nothing more than three portable toilets lined up next to each other. Carla had stared at them for entirely too long while she scribbled her chicken-scratch note. But, the woman she'd seen going in to the middle stall had such impeccable tits that Carla couldn't help thinking about how it would feel to bury her face in between them.

She imagined the other woman's cloth draped hardened nipples softly grazing her face. She'd breathe in softly before unbuttoning just the top two buttons of this beautiful woman's blouse, freeing the left breast from the bra it was trapped in and taking as much of it as possible into her mouth. Carla could feel her panties moistening at the thought. If there was a way to fuck someone inside of an outdoor toilet, she'd have to figure it out before she lost her nerve. She held the note in her hand and read it to herself one last time, just to be sure, "Wet kitty, stuck behind the water slide." That was a subtle enough statement she figured.

She wondered who would meet her this time, and hoped she'd be able to break her previous record. There was something about carnivals that, without failure always sent her hormones into overdrive. Right now she wanted a penis as fat as a tree trunk to spread her walls apart and explode with milky goodness inside of her; she wanted someone's hot juicy pussy lips inside her mouth. She'd tried, tried to coach herself out of the habit, tried to convince herself that she could just go to the carnival like everyone else and enjoy the rides.

However, going down the water slide only made her think of going down on a sloppy wet pussy, the ring toss made her feel like she was landing cock rings on an assorted array of hardened dicks. She didn't even want to think about the time she tried eating a chili-cheese dog hoping it would quell her hunger for a hot dick in her mouth. None of it worked, she needed a lay or several of them and she needed it as soon as possible.

She waited in her car parked directly behind the water slide keeping an eye out for anyone who might have been looking for her. After an hour, nothing happened. The only thing getting wet was her car from the back-splash created by people on the slide. She waited an hour again and the sun began to set. The carnival would close in another hour. No one was coming, especially not Carla. She'd never had such bad luck at this. But, she figured, when you want something done right best to just do it yourself. Turning the radio on, she pushed the seat back and thought about the woman from before. Before long she felt her panties getting wet again. She slipped her hands to her sides and fumbled around with the clasped hook on her pants before finally getting it to unhook. Her fingers gripped the zipper and slid it down gently. A wave of relief came over Carla as she was finally able to touch the soft lace of her underwear. She slipped one hand down and stroked at her pussy gently letting herself feel the growing wetness soaking through the fabric of her panties. Her other hand gripped on to the headrest.

She stroked at her lips until her fingers were soaked with sweaty pussy juice and she couldn't resist the urge to slip her fingers into her mouth and taste her own goodness. First just one finger, twirled around in her mouth like a lollipop. The taste was too good to resist and she instinctively took the rest into her mouth licking and sucking at them like a hungry cat. Before long she'd shimmied her way out of her panties. She couldn't resist by now. Her clit was throbbing and begging for skin to skin contact. She tried to go slowly, just petting at first. But it seemed despite herself she'd slipped a finger in anyway. She was drenched and the feeling of a single digit sliding in and out as her wall clenched up desperate to hold it inside made her blind with desire for cum. She slipped another finger in and gradually increased the frequency of her strokes. Carla seemed possessed now. She moved her other hand from the headrest down to her heaving bosom. Slipping it under her bra she massaged her breasts tenderly, pinching at her already erect nipples so that they grew rock hard.

For a moment she wished she'd succeeded in finding a partner, she wished there'd been someone there to suck and bite at her nipples the way she liked. She slipped a third finger in and imagined taking a massive cock in her mouth as she went in and out of herself. In and out, in and out her fingers moved in unison, slightly curled inside of her. She felt her breath hitching and her pelvis arching upward involuntarily. She was close, so desperately close. She should have been within one or two strokes, she should have been able to get herself there. But her mind was fixated now; she was stuck on the edge unable to cum and desperate for a massive shaft to finish her off. Sighing in frustration she pulled her pants back on and put the driver's seat back in its proper position. When she looked up she saw a piece of paper stuck to her windshield. How long had it been there, she didn't recall seeing it before. It didn't matter, the thought of someone seeing her, watching her, only made Carla's excitement grow. She stepped out of her car and walked around to the front of her car Grabbing the note from her windshield she read out loud "Slow day. Staff's gone fish'n. Meet us at the hall of mirrors." Whoever wrote it didn't bother signing their names.

Carla briefly wondered about the "us" part of things. But the hope of finding a helpful dick to come to her rescue pushed all other thoughts to the side. Walking up to the fence she saw that the park had in fact closed early for the day. With everything blocked off, the only way for her to get back in was to climb over the metal fence. She didn't have any trouble getting up, but in her haste to get her pants back on she'd forgotten to put her panties back on. She tossed one leg over the other side so that she sat straddling the top bar. She could feel the cold metal sliding against her pussy lips through the thin fabric of her pants. Dear lord, it felt so good to her. She sat for a while sliding back and forth on the top rail and touching herself wildly. She could sense her pants were now embarrassingly wet, but Carla didn't give a damn. She kept on sliding up against the cold hard metal pole rubbing at her pussy wildly. She reached down past the hem of her pants and ravenously inspected the results of her work. She was beyond delighted with herself when she softly grazed her pussy lips and felt herself swimming in a pool of sweet secretions. Finally hopping over the fence, she pulled her hand out and sucked her fingers dry one more time.

The Hall of mirrors wasn't really a hall. It was simply a parked trailer that had been painted with all sorts of wonky colors. She looked around but couldn't find anybody. Maybe it was just a prank. But she'd already gone through all the trouble, she figured she might as well go inside and make sure. She stepped in and was immediately greeted by her own figure looking back at her. In every direction an endless line of mirror reflections were staring back at her. She took in the site. Her pussy soaked pants, her top that now hung loosely around her glistening breasts, her perpetually erect nipples. Her dark brown hair now comfortably tussled. She looked as fuckable as she felt.

Walking around a bit, she tried to find someone, anyone. "Hello?" she finally called out. No one responded. She tried again anyway. "Hello!" Again, no response was given. She was just about to leave, she'd turned and was headed back toward the door when she felt a hand grab her and pull her in the opposite direction. A mirror just to her side revealed the oblong figure of a man with bulging biceps standing just behind her. He wore an undershirt and a tight pair of jeans. His hair was curly and cut short almost like a Caesar cut.

"What's your name?" Carla muttered out, but the guy wouldn't give it to her. He simply took her hand and guided it toward the crotch of his jeans.

"You want it?" he asked, his voice deep and resonating. Carla nodded her confirmation and followed him back into the maze of mirrors. He stopped at a spot where the mirrors seemed to stretch their figures out so that they both looked about ten feet tall. Carla watched as his large muscular hands suddenly grabbed at her crotch.

"You're already wet" he chuckled. "She's already wet boys." As Carla looked on in confused wonder, two more figures stepped out. They all looked alike, except for their haircuts. One had grown his hair out and pulled it back into a ponytail, the other had a completely shaven head. She understood now. They were the trapeze trio. The bald one and the one with the ponytail seemed to be taking orders from the curly haired one. He'd been smiling deviously at Carla, then as if arriving at a plan he pushed one of them forward toward her and demanded that he start. It was the bald one and Carla stared at him in confusion until he managed to explain things to her. "You have to say you want it."

She looked at the bulging package that awaited her and smiled, "I really, really want it." She said, grabbing for his junk. But he shoved her hand away. "Naw, you gotta say what you want too." Looking at all three of them with an immeasurable amount of lust Carla spoke up. "I want all three of you to fuck me like a dirty slut. I want your cum all over me now!"

The curly haired one spoke up again. "You heard the bitch Nicky, give her what she wants." Without any further delay, Nicky grabbed Carla's face and guided her down to her knees. He shoved his jeans clad crotch at her mouth and Carla eagerly licked at it, feeling the outline of his balls against her tongue. He undid his fly so that his junk hung out and she could feel more of him inside of her. Then as she'd taken his entire nut sack he shoved her face into his crotch and held it there. He pulled away while Carla desperately tried to find her way back to his dick.

"Damn, you really are a whore" he teased before stepping out of his pants and revealing his massive cock to her. Carla licked at the tip playfully before taking as much as possible into her mouth and letting Nicky fuck her throat. Suddenly, she felt a familiar hand grabbing at her crotch again. "Lay her down" came another order. "Her pussy wants it bad." Just like that she was on her back with her legs spread apart. Nicky knelt beside her and returned his cock to its rightful place inside her mouth. Those hands, the familiar ones were now deep inside her pussy thrusting in and out. After a while Nicky stepped away and the curly haired one just as quickly barked out another order.

"Tommy, it's your turn" he instructed the bald one. Tommy made quick work of removing his pants and getting his dick out which Carla thankfully accepted into her mouth. Meanwhile She felt a face being shoved down toward her muff licking its way past her pussy lips and eating her juices vigorously. It was amazing, in every direction all she could see was row after row reflections of herself being screwed in all different directions. Still, she wished one of them would finally put her clit out of its misery and stick their shaft inside of her. While Tommy was thrusting in and out of her mouth intermittently teasing her face with his stiffy, Carla finally pleaded. "Please, I want it inside me now!"

Nicky stood off in the corner stroking himself. He looked at Carla, studying her face for the appropriate amount of desperation. "Danny, maybe we ought to let her have it" he teased.

"Not yet" The curly haired one insisted while guiding Carla's hand toward her pussy and instructing that she touch herself while he continued to eat her box. She complied without questioning. Meanwhile Tommy and Nicky were now taking turns in her mouth. She felt Danny's hands going up her body grabbing at her breasts and she continued to rub her pussy. There was so much pussy juice and she desperately wanted to taste it. But any time she moved her hands away from her clit, someone grabbed them and placed them right back down. She was acting outside of herself now just desperate to cum no matter what it took. Her eyes glazed over reflecting nothing but lust and desire which Danny must have noticed because he finally relented. He grabbed at her legs and put her knees up just a little.

Tommy and Nicky stepped aside and Danny shoved his tongue into Carla's mouth. "You like the way your pussy taste in my mouth?" Danny asked.

"It's so good" Carla gasped. He smiled with satisfaction.

"You want my dick in your pussy?" Carla tried no to seem too eager, but she couldn't help it. He was straddling her now and Tommy and Nicky stood off to either side of her face stroking their dicks and waiting for whatever was coming next.

"Yes please. Please I want that fat cock inside me. I want all three of you to tear my fucking clit up. Give it to me. Please." She licked at Tommy's dick then Nicky's.

"Please, I need your giant pole inside my clit." With another smile, Danny undid his pants and revealed the biggest dick Carla had ever seen. He first teased her with it. Sliding it up and down her lips before he gently guided his shaft inside of her. Carla didn't know if she could handle it all. He was only half way in and if was starting to feel tight. Her walls throbbed harder and harder as he pumped in and out of her. She stopped thinking about it. She wanted all of him, every last inch. She turned her head toward Tommy and took his cock in her mouth again. It was dripping now with salty pre cum and she went crazy at the sensation of it dripping down her throat. She could tell he was close to shooting off in her mouth the thought of his cum excited her, but he pulled away. Danny was pumping in and out of her furiously. She felt her walls swelling again. If he kept up his pace she'd cum in no time. She grabbed for Nicky and took his balls in her mouth licking at them before guiding her lips up to the tip of his dick. She had him inside her mouth now and was letting him take control of things. He shoved his entire cock in her mouth so that Carla could feel him hitting the back of her throat. Suddenly, Carla felt her entire body seize up then rapidly relax. Her once throbbing pussy suddenly exploded with relief and began rhythmically pulsating. She'd cum, and now her cum juices were dripping out of her pussy and down her legs.

Danny tried to keep going but the sensitivity of her walls wouldn't allow him. He pulled out and began jerking off with his dick aimed squarely at Carla's chest. He shot off and his creamy load landed directly in the center of Carla's midsection pooling around her belly button. When he'd finished he instructed the other two to do the same. Then he stepped over and let Carla lick his dick clean while the other two continued jerking off. Tommy and Nicky finally unloaded all over her now cream covered belly. With that all three stepped away finding their pants and leaving without another word.

Carla lay there basking in satisfaction she felt a confused mix of relief and eagerness to find another person to fuck. Gathering her things, she got dressed and walked out back toward her car. She passed Tommy on her way out, he was still locking up.

"Which one of you found my note?" She inquired out of curiosity. Tommy looked puzzled.

"What note?"

"Well, how did you know I…"

"Oh, my buddy Nicky saw you in the car. He told me and Danny you'd be in to it." Tommy waved her off saying that if they didn't finish locking up they'd be in big trouble. Carla made her way back to her car a little disappointed. Maybe her note had been too subtle, maybe it blew off in the wind. She was in the parking lot now getting ready to head back to her apartment when someone called out again. She turned in the darkness to see that it was the woman from before.

"I'm sorry; I've just been out here for a while. I was hoping someone could help me. I can't get my car to start." Carla thought for a second. The carnival must have been closed for over an hour by this point. Why didn't she just call a cab?

"I don't have any jumper cables or anything, sorry…"

But the other woman was persistent. "Well, maybe you could just give me a ride? I swear I am not crazy." All Carla could think about was burying her face in this other woman's ample chest.

Despite her better judgment she found herself saying "okay." The next thing she knew, Carla was inside her car with a gorgeous red head staring her down. She was covered in cum, and hoped the other woman wouldn't notice. She just had to get the key in the ignition and drive; it wasn't that big a deal.

She got her car keys out and the other woman introduced herself as Rachel, everything was going just fine. And then it happened. Rachel had been moving around in her seat uncomfortably.

"I feel like I'm sitting on something" she explained. Then she reached under and pulled out Carla's panties, she'd been sitting on Carla's completely soaked underwear and was now looking for an explanation.

"What is this?"

Carla was desperate for a reasonable explanation, but also horny as hell. She figured what the heck; she might as well tell the truth. There was nothing wrong with a woman who liked sex. "Those are mine." Rachel held them up with one finger as if studying them. Carla tried to concentrate on other things. She put her key in the ignition and attempted starting the car, but she was stopped. Great, she thought. She'd gone too far this time and now she was going to hear about it from a complete stranger. Rachel felt at the fabric again.

"They're kind of damp." She sniffed at them "and dirty too." But she did not look displeased. She placed a hand on top of Carla's then reached into her purse and pulled out a napkin.

"I think this is yours too," she explained while handing it over, it was the note from earlier. Carla got the message. Carla took the key out and tossed them behind her She turned toward Rachel, a knowing expression on her face. She should have gone for a kiss but couldn't take her mind off of those giant melons bursting out of Rachel's blouse. They felt fantastic, like two rounded pillows pushing up against her face. Rachel made quick work of removing her shirt and bra and Carla just as quickly took one breast in her mouth biting and sucking desperately at the other woman's nipple. After a few seconds she felt something sweet gushing out into her mouth.

"What the hell is that?" she panted out. "You're lactating?" Rachel nodded in confirmation then looked to Carla to see if she was alright with it. Carla said nothing; she simply went back to sucking alternating between the left and the right jug enjoying the milky surprise that came with her efforts. Rachel had already undone Carla's pants and was busying herself with massaging her already plump pussy walls.

"Oh, you're so wet" she moaned. "Oh, my god you're so wet." She pulled Carla's face away from her chest and up toward her own then kissed her softly before bossily instructing.

"Take off your pants." Carla pushed the driver's seat back again and did as she was told. Pushing her own seat back so that they were in the same position Rachel leaned over and whispered "sit on my face." Carla hesitated, but Rachel wanted it more than ever now.

"I want your sweaty slut juices all over my face." She pushed the seat as far back as it would go.

"Come on, sit on my face. Your pussy's so plump and ripe like a peach. I just want it on my face so bad." Lifting one leg over Rachel's lap, Carla made her way to the other woman's face and sat down pushing her muff toward Rachel's eager-to-please lips. She rocked back and forth as she felt Rachel's tongue darting around in a circular motion licking at the wetness coming from her inner walls. She felt her one hand slipping down a trembling thigh and up into a skirt where she was greeted by Rachel's soaking wet panties. She slipped them off and stuffed them into her mouth licking at the center and taking in as much wetness as she could. Carla loved the taste of other people's pussy. Rachel's tasted fruit and between that and her giant milk jugs Carla couldn't get enough of her. She rubbed a finger against Rachel's clit sliding up and down before teasing her way inside. Carla sat up just slightly while Rachel licked playfully at her thighs. Rachel wanted her to stay, but Carla had decided to take control of things. She moved her body down and kneelt in front of Rachel's lap so that she could bury her head inside of Rachel's skirt. She slipped finger back inside and felt immediately welcomed. Then she licked at Rachel's now exposed clit and began massaging her own throbbing pussy.

"Did I make you wet?" she teased as Rachel's hips bucked upward involuntarily. She followed Rachel's body with her mouth as the other woman squirmed with pleasure. She grabbed at her hips to keep Rachel from moving away and went after her sucking her lips into her mouth and licking at her clit unrelentingly.

"Oh God!" Rachel yelped. She was almost there she just needed a little bit more. "Put them all inside me. Oh. Mmh, I want all your fingers in me now." Carla did as she was told slipping one finger in at a time. She then took her time sliding her whole hand in and out slowly increasing her speed and marveling at how tightly Rachel's walls squeezed around her hand. After a while the red head grabbed at Carla's hair and pulled her away motioning for her to sit back in the driver's seat.

"I wanna cum on your face" she explained. With Rachel standing over her rubbing away at her clit, Carla began teasing her own clit again. She felt her lips swelling, she tried to hold off so that they would cum together, but she saw Rachel's eyes go blank and she knew it was too late. Rachel's pussy juice came squirting out of her like warm spurts of sticky liquid all over Carla's face. It was startling, but she kept her focus and continued stroking at her aching clit while Rachel's body collapsed on top of her, shaking with ecstasy.

Rachel slipped her hand down to join Carla's and joined in. Before long Carla had cum too. They took turns feeding each other their cum juices while their bodies fell into a natural rhythm rubbing up against each other so that their still pulsing clits slid up and down the other woman's inner thigh releasing even more pleasure and sending their bodies into overdrive. They fell asleep like that; naked and spooning under the glow of the carnival lights. As Carla drifted off, she promised herself next time she'd get more people. Ten at least, maybe even twenty. There was just something about a good carnival cum. She couldn't wait for the next one.

www.ingramcontent.com/pod-product-compliance
Lightning Source LLC
Chambersburg PA
CBHW072052150726
47999CB00002B/998